# Night Terrors

Written by: Amy Beth Zickefoose

*To my amazing husband who always believed I could accomplish this dream and drove me to do the very best that I possibly could. You will always be my rock.*

# Chapter 1

Tick, tick, tick, tick, tick, tick. The sound of that stupid thing with balls on my therapist's desk was driving me nuts. Who needs one of those? They say it's supposed to be calming, relieve stress, but to me? It made me want to pick up everything off her desk and throw it out the first window that I came to. Dr. Thompson was her name. This was the third therapist I had been assigned in 3 months by my primary care doctor. I have been told on multiple occasions that I had a rough time with commitment when it came to therapists. Coming from my background, I don't think anyone could blame me for my outlook on life and the people in it, or how I decided to fit them into my life. People took a backseat to me, especially when they were trying to give me advice on my situation that they hadn't had to live through.

I was 26 years old. Dropped out of college, and newly divorced by a man that had nothing better to do in our married life than torture me and cause me pain, both physically and mentally. Does that mean I want to talk about it to some woman or man who has no idea what I went through and just sits there with that blank look on their face judging me for every move that I made during the 5 years of that marriage? No. I want nothing to do with this. My primary care doctor, Doctor Baker, convinced me to give it a try. She had been seeing me as a patient for years and she played a big part in breaking me free from the hell that particular relationship and life decision had left me in physically.

I have been suffering from night terrors ever since the incident that led to me leaving him for good and the police putting him behind bars. I thought they would stop with time or at least fade a bit, but they just got worse. Every time I lay down to sleep, my mind becomes a world of its own, and there is no telling what terror might face me. It got to a point where I decided I would do anything to stay awake. I took up running, writing, reading everything I could find, working an online job that allowed me to work weird hours overnight, and trying to forget that I live in this city by myself with no family and one friend along with my dog, Fritz.

Fritz was my best friend as of late, then there was Don the bar owner that loves me despite myself. I don't think you can count a doctor that you don't know the first name of as a friend, or I would add Doctor Baker to the list as well just to prove I'd been trying. In reality, I hadn't been trying, and I hadn't attempted to reconnect with friends or family since the incident. I kept to myself, and I enjoyed it enough to get by without being too awfully depressed. Fritz and I would go on runs together. I talked to him all the time, and he kept all my secrets. After the *incident* left me suffering a traumatic brain injury, everything had changed. I had a metal plate in my head, migraines constantly, and recurring night terrors, but I walked away with my life, so that's something, right? That's what the therapists and the doctor want to focus on, the fact that I got away with my life. To me, that wasn't an accomplishment. It was simply survival. There I was a year later, and I was still barely surviving.

Apparently, I had been ignoring Dr. Thompson, because as if to break my train of thought, she cleared her throat almost too loudly and choked herself. I sat there waiting for her to finish her coughing fit and regain her composure, while also trying to keep my composure. It had also been told to me that I laughed at inappropriate moments, but sometimes people made it too easy to be entertained. Finally, when she was breathing normally again, she said "Delaney, listen, please stop focusing on all the negative that you faced. There is more to life than what you went through and the discomfort and disabilities it has caused." I raised an eyebrow in her direction. "I'm sorry, I was unaware that I was *disabled*. Could you put that in writing so I can get a check from someone somewhere? I thought you were here to assist in me getting better, not point out that I am not the person I was. I am struggling, but I'm surviving, and doing a pretty good job of at least that." She looked down at the papers in her hands that held some undisclosed information about what she thought of me. "Delaney, I apologize if you found offense in that statement, but no, to answer your question, I cannot sign anything saying you are disabled mentally, because you aren't. Now how about you answer one of my questions? What do you think is the particular reason that you cannot move on from the accident that resulted in your injury? What is keeping you so angry?" I smiled contemptuously. "Is that a serious question, doc? So, for arguments sake, say the *accident* you are referring to happened to you instead of me? Would you shake it off, jump up, and thank me for giving you a reason to find the strength to keep trying in life? Or, possibly, would it make you angry enough and scar you enough that you would have issues with people and moving on toward a *normal* life?"

"You know," she snapped, "someone could really take offense to how you speak to them. You should watch your tone and how you approach people."

"Doc," I said as I picked up my purse and put on my jacket, "I could not care less whether anyone takes offense or not when I'm telling the truth. If you don't want a truthful answer, maybe you shouldn't ask any questions to begin with. I don't think this is a good fit, and I think I'm going to be looking for a different therapist or just tackling my issues on my own. None of you can seem to understand how to *help* me, so maybe I just can't be helped. Thank you for your time, I guess. I just gave you a good 45 minutes back free to use toward another paying customer. Hopefully you will put more effort into helping them than you did me. You can mail me my final bill."

With that snarky remark, I walked out the door. I had had enough therapy for the foreseeable future. Talking about my *disabilities* and *discomfort* wouldn't make them go away. It honestly just lights a fire in me. I wasn't always this way, someone made me this way. Yet, here I stand, the only one picking up the pieces and trying to fit jagged part with jagged part to make my life somewhat livable again. The sun was blinding, and my head was throbbing, so I put on my shades and picked up the pace just to try to burn off some of the steam and pressure building.

Dr. Baker was going to be mad at my next appointment. I truly just don't think therapy will ever help me. What was wrong with me went deeper than some mental issues. It was physical, mental, and the result of some abusive alcoholic making sure that I could never be normal again. Dr. Baker had also told

7

me to write down my night terrors to help me hopefully work through them. I intended to begin that whenever I decided I just had to sleep. Usually, as soon as I woke, I worked as hard as I could at forgetting them. At that point, I believed I could stay awake at least 16 more hours.

Given the crappy day I had, I decided to stop at Don's and grab a beer. I liked Don's because nobody else liked Don's. Most days when I visited Don's, it was quiet, and we could sit and talk about whatever we would like. When I first started frequenting Don's, I sat alone at the bar and wouldn't speak. He soon got me to where I'd chat about light things like the weather, Fritz, a football game, or something that was menial and not important in the grand scheme of things. Don worked hard at winning me over and getting me more comfortable with speaking to him. Pretty soon, we knew all each other's pasts, pain, and we were still comfortable together. He told me I was like the daughter he never had, and half the time I thought he was poking fun but the other half of the time I knew he was dead serious. He loved me, and I loved him, though neither of us would say it. He was like the Dad I needed to get me through day to day with advice, handyman situations, and most importantly just an ear to listen to me on the rare occasions I found myself wanting to speak to someone other than Fritz.

That day, I walked in, and Don's was packed as opposed to its normal 2 or 3 patrons including myself. There were at least 10 people in there. Some playing pool, some drinking at the bar, and a few of them were playing the jukebox. I walked up to the corner of the bar and found a seat far enough away that I felt I looked

8

inapproachable. Don walked over with my go-to beer and told me he would put my order of fries in for me. I couldn't figure out if that was a compliment or just sad, but I told him thank you anyway.

"What are all these people doing here?" I asked while glancing around at all the faces that were new and only a couple that were regulars. "Contrary to what you might believe," Don said, "I do like to make money in this place. I ran a special that if you brought someone, your drinks were half off from 10AM to 3PM. Thought maybe that would get me more business throughout the day, and apparently it is working. Don't seem so bummed about it, Delaney." "I'm not bummed," I spat out, though I was incredibly bummed, "thanks for the beer." He looked at me through tired but intelligent eyes and sighed. "Why don't you bring one of your friends in? I never see you with anyone and I worry about you," I looked up at him. "I don't have any friends, Don. None except you, and I don't believe seeing you at your own bar would earn me the discount," I answered while grinning at the old man. He always knew when I was making a joke, but he seemed less amused than normal, probably because of all these people milling around. He was easy to be around and had a rough past like myself. He never forced me to say more than I wanted to and was the best at gauging when it was better not to talk to me at all.

"You have to have some friends, Delaney," he replied while looking sad. I hated sympathy. I didn't want it and didn't need it. I needed someone that could just exist in the same room with me without making me feel like I needed to try too hard, but therapy had left me in a mood, so I shook it off. He was just looking out for me. "I used to. I used to have a lot of friends before I got married. I haven't even tried to reconnect with them since the divorce. I figured if they wanted to see me, they knew where to find me, at least in theory, though none of them have attempted to find me yet that I know of. I used to have a best friend named Lane. He was pretty cool. We met when we were kids and grew up together. He hated my ex, so he dropped me like a hot potato the second we got married. I hate my ex too, but I guess it's as they say, hindsight is 20 / 20." Don looked pleased at the prospect of me having someone I *could* count as a friend. "Why don't you call him?" asked Don. I looked down at my fries that were just not hitting the spot tonight. "I don't even know if he has the same number, Don. He also probably doesn't want to hear from me. I can't imagine I'd make very good company these days." "Delaney, having your only friend as an old barkeep isn't really the only option you have at your age. Put some effort in, please?" "I'll think about it, Don."

After my reply, Don just nodded and walked off. He had a couple eyeing him at the bar that were needing attended to. That got me thinking about Lane. I wondered where the heck he could be and if he was happy? Or maybe he was just as miserable as I was and could use a friend to talk to. I decided to mull it over on whether I should contact him or not. It probably couldn't hurt anything except my pride to try to call him, but I wasn't sure I was ready for that just yet. I had about 4 more beers and ate my fries, then took off to walk home to Fritz.

I worked part time transcribing documents for a doctor's office in town. It was all online, so I really made my own hours. This worked perfectly because I could work all night. About 3:30 AM my eyes were growing heavy, so I went to the fridge and got an energy drink and chugged it. I sat on the couch and scooped Fritz up and snuggled him a bit then tried to get him to play with me to keep me up. Fritz was a small dog, weighing in about 28 lbs. dripping wet, and was part chihuahua and part long-haired something. He was a mutt, but he was my mutt. He didn't really look like a chihuahua or act like one. He was calm, chill, and he didn't like loud noises, but he loved me.

I wasn't ready to sleep. Even when I did sleep, it never felt like I rested. Imagine wrestling a gorilla all night then having to be around people the next day. I could blame my night terrors for my attitude, but really my attitude just sucked these days. I continued to work and about 5 AM, it was growing to be too much, and I tossed in the towel. I laid down in bed and hoped for the best, but mentally I was preparing for the worst. I never knew what journey my mind would take me on while my eyes were closed. There was no escaping it, as the body eventually had to sleep. I gave in and closed my eyes, begrudgingly.

I woke with tears in my eyes and a migraine that could knock a giant on its butt. I grabbed Fritz to hug him and wrote the night terror in its entirety.

### *The Strain*

*There had been a pandemic, a plague of sorts, that had been in our country for years now. I had lost my job as a banker when they went entirely online due to the circumstances and took a job as a prop* coordinator for a movie set.  All was going to hell, but they were still making movies.  Priorities, right?

The movie set I was working on was for a film that was taking place in and on the ocean.  We, of course, were filming in a body of water, but I would not call it an ocean even though technically it was part of the ocean.  It was a large cove with an amusement park on one side with shops that have been abandoned for close to five years on the other.  They edited all the background out except the amusement park that was supposed to be on the beach in the actual film.

That particular day was chilly, and I felt bad for the actress that had to spend the day half-clothed and half-submerged in the freezing water.  I got a text on my phone and made sure nobody was looking as I read it.  My friend Lane was really upset and said he needed to see me as soon as possible.  There were hundreds of people on the set already and it was growing dark, so I told him the address where he could find me.

I noticed his old car pull up and snuck over to get his attention.  As he got out, I immediately noticed several things were off.  His eyes were pitch black, even the white part.  His mouth was in a smile that looked like a grimace, almost like it was painful for him.  He had lost about 30 pounds since I'd seen him two weeks ago, which I thought to be next to impossible as he was never a big guy.  I took a step back and raised my gaze to meet his eyes again.

He approached and with the odd smile on his face told me that something was wrong through gritted teeth.  "I don't know what is happening to me.  A week ago, I woke up and things started changing.  I can see things that I normally couldn't, and the light is killing me. I can't stop smiling if that is what you can call what my face is doing right now. I am scared to go to the Doctor because if this has something to do with the pandemic, they will take me away. What do I do? Have you seen anyone else like me? I'm freaking out a bit, D. I don't know how to handle this or what to do next."

Other than his voice and his clothes, he barely resembled the friend I knew a couple of weeks ago. He was in distress, and I had no idea how to help him. "There have been talks about a new strain. Do you think that's what this is? I haven't seen anyone that had the symptoms you have, but I don't really see many people except here at work, and they all seem to look fairly normal." He replied, "I have no idea. The change wasn't sudden, but it was fast. I don't feel right. I can't eat because I'm not hungry, I can't sleep because my eyes are killing me, and I can't figure out what I'm supposed to do about my body having a mind of its own! I feel like it just keeps getting worse and building up to something, but I don't know what."

My first thought was, this was not good, but it wasn't terrible. We would figure something out. As it grew darker out, I saw more people coming onto the set. There were a lot of black eyes and a lot of smiling faces. In fact, it looked like I was the only one in view that didn't have the symptoms. For the first time that week we were staying late to shoot after sundown. Lane noticed the same thing and it seemed like his smile grew bigger. I wasn't sure if he felt reassured to see more people that looked like him, or if he was just happy that the sun was going down, and the pain subsiding. Either way, I think we were both hoping that one of the *people walking around would have more answers than we had.*

*He reached out and stopped someone. "When did you start to change?" The young man replied, "Three days ago, man. What about you?" to which Lane replied, "A week ago, give or take." "Have you heard anything about what it is or what's happening to us?" The man looked at us with a puzzled grimace on his face. "No. Nobody seems to have any answers or anything that they have found that could help. It's frustrating in this day and age that nobody has any answers at all, somebody must know something and be able to do something about it. I just don't know where to find a person that would have the resources without getting locked away somewhere and used as an experiment, ya know?" "Same here. Thanks for the information and good luck! I hope we get answers from someone quickly, it's miserable."*

*I was just standing there in awe. I was surrounded by these people with black eyes wearing gruesome smiles and couldn't figure out whether I should run or try to assist. I couldn't leave Lane, so I stayed by his side. I believe it made him feel better to know that he was not alone. The least I could do was walk with him and let him talk and see if we could hash out a plan together.*

*I looped my arm into Lane's as we walked through the crowd of faces. Everyone seemed in decent health and walking along as if they had somewhere important to be, despite their current state. Then things took a turn for the worst. It started with a man collapsing. A crowd gathered around him and hovered almost as soon as he hit the ground. We ran over to see what the issue was, and his eyes were leaking black liquid and his face was frozen in a gruesome smile. I asked the crowd to move back and give him space, and almost every face staring back at me had leaking eyes and dead-like faces. I knelt next to the man that had fallen and tried to check for a pulse, but when I touched him, it was like his body was stone. He was hard to the touch and colder than he should have been even if he had died on contact with where he lay. There was no pulse. There was no movement. There was no breath. He was stuck in time in this terrifying way.*

*Lane looked at me and at that moment his eyes started leaking the fluid. It looked like black tears, but they were coming fast and streaking down his face and onto his shirt and even reaching his pants and flowing to the ground. The liquid showed no signs of stopping its flow from his black eyes. Looking at the crowd there were so many people with black streaking down their face that I could not make out anyone who didn't have this awful untimely death happening to them. It appears I was all alone again, and I was helpless. Lane started to fall to the ground, and I got underneath him, but he was too heavy for me to hold up. I fell to the ground underneath him, then rolled out carefully placing him on the ground. I knelt there with him as he took a few more agonizing breaths and then they ceased. In fact, everything ceased. I heard no birds, no crickets, no waves, there was just nothing. It was like he took the entire living world with him on his journey to the other side with that final breath.*

*I looked up and realized I was the only one left alive on the movie set that just moments ago was bustling with crowds heading in different directions.*

*Nobody was around and there wasn't a sound made except my cries and my screams for help. There were no sirens, no ambulances, and no fire trucks. Nobody came to help. Nobody came to save my best friend or console me in my grief. If this was the new strain, was I alone? Had I been exposed? Where do I go from here? If I was exposed, was I going to die alone in the same way that I had just experienced all these unfortunate deaths?*

*A massive dog approached me from behind one of the funnel-cake stands and nuzzled up to my arm. I looked over and reached out and put my arm around his thick neck while pulling him close and sobbing into his soft white fur. He let me cry it out, then brought his head up and tried to lick my tears away. I recognized him as the director's Great Pyrenees names Duke. I pulled his face close to mine, and in the dim light, his fur looked black in spots. I pulled him even closer, and he sat, and I realized the dark spots were where I had been sobbing in his fur. I grabbed Duke's leash that was hanging slack and stood and decided if I was going to die, I wasn't going to go out laying down. I would take one last walk as far as my legs would carry me. As we were walking, I reached down and patted Duke on the head. When I looked up, it felt like my entire body was stuck in cement. I just stopped. Breathing stopped, hope stopped, forward motion stopped. I fell to the ground like a stone and Duke lay beside me as I accepted my fate on the cold concrete staring up at the beautiful night sky for a few seconds before all turned to black.*

# Chapter 2

Apparently, Don had made me think of Lane, which explains why he was the main character in my night terror. Maybe I should call him. Enough time had passed that it would most likely be fine, and he probably wouldn't hate me. There is a chance he would still hate me, though. That thought put a knot in my stomach. I guess I wouldn't know until I dial the number, right? I sat there reasoning with myself for a while on the pros and cons and gave up and finally dialed the number from a very old memory, but still in the front of my mind.

"Hello?" He sounded annoyed as he clipped the hello as short and uninviting as he could. There's a chance he had gotten a lot of robocalls or something, and maybe that's why he sounded so angry. "Hey, Lane. Sorry. I probably shouldn't have called. It's been too long. How are you?" I sputtered out like a person that belongs in an insane asylum. I'm not sure what was going through my head, but as if to clear it up I smacked my hand to my forehead as soon as I stopped sputtering nonsense. "Uh, who is this?" He asked. Crap. It never occurred to me to say my name, which earned me another forehead smack from myself. Shake it off, D. I had to start making sense or he was going to hang up on me. "Delaney. From school? I knew I shouldn't have called. I have no idea what I was thinking. Don mentioned that I should have friends, and you were the only person that really came to mind." "Hey! Stop for a second. Delaney Jameson?" He asked. "Yeah, Delaney. That's me." I said sheepishly. I knew he lived up here in Tulsa just from people talking occasionally. We both grew up in a small town with not much to do, but neither of us really wanted to stay there indefinitely.

"Oh, wow. I was just talking about you yesterday to Mom. She misses you by the way. How the hell have you been?" He actually sounded excited when he asked that. I wasn't sure how I was going to go into the next part. Nobody but Don had asked me how I was in a very long time that didn't have a doctorate in Psychology or medicine. I decided to go with the most vague answer I could come up with and hope for the best. "Me? I've been okay. Working a lot. I have a dog. His name is Fritz." He interrupted, "You still in Tulsa?" "Yeah. Still here. I live about a block from Don's which is my excuse for that being the only place I go besides the doctor. How have you been?" He hesitated. That wasn't like him. Usually, you couldn't shut Lane up even if you wanted to. "Well, I've been better. I haven't been feeling too hot lately. Something seems to be going bad with my eyes. I haven't wanted to go to the doctor again, because I'm kind of scared of what they are going to say to me. Other than that, though, I'm okay. Keeping a smile plastered to my face and showing every day who is boss, like always."

My stomach turned. His eyes? Something was wrong with his eyes? He had a smile plastered on his face? I'm seriously losing it, I thought. He is messing with me. Some way somehow, he knew what I faced last night and was poking fun at it. But how could he possibly know? How could anyone possibly know? There is no way anyone could have told him because the only thing I'd done is write it down and I could still see my journal in front of me. I have got to stop being so paranoid, but something seemed very off. I got goosebumps up and down my spine, curled up with Fritz, and decided I better keep talking or he would hang up. I wasn't used to talking on the phone to regular people without it having to do with ordering food.

"What's wrong with your eyes? Do they just hurt?" I blurted out. "Nah, they started getting really dark. I think my pupil keeps growing. I can see everything better, but only in the dark. The light kills me. Hey! How about I meet you at Don's tonight? We can have a burger and hang out like old times. It would do me good to get away from Mom for a little bit. She moved in with me for a while to help me since I started having the issues with my eyes. Maybe Don wouldn't think you needed friends if you showed up with one!" He sounded so excited, there was no way I could turn him down, even as skeptical as I was. "Alright. It should be dark by around 8:30 tonight. Want to meet then?" I asked. "Sure," he paused again, "just please take into consideration it's been years since you have seen me, and time isn't always kind to us. I don't look much like the person you used to know, but I'm doing the best with what I've got. I really missed you, Delaney. I know I shouldn't have, but I asked around about you a lot after the accident. I knew you would call when you were ready, but I honestly didn't think it would take you this long. I'm so sorry it came to that. I'm glad that creep got what he deserved, though." "Yeah, let's just act like that creep never existed, and go back to how we used to be tonight. Does that sound like a plan? I'll send you directions to Don's." I knew he probably knew where Don's was, but at the same time I didn't want to stay on that line of conversation. "Yeah. The best plan. I'll see you later," and with that he hung up the phone.

19

There was no way that was a coincidence. Time hadn't been kind to him? How could it be that his eyes are blackened, he can't be out in the sunlight, time hadn't been kind to him, and he was plastering a smile on his face? I couldn't believe that I had dreamt that last night along with my own demise, and he just happened to be having all the same issues that appeared in the dream. It didn't make sense. Please let this be a coincidence, I thought. Please just let it be some eye crap going around, and for God's sake, please give me a better ending than I got last night.

At a quarter to eight, I was pacing. I had no idea what to wear when I was actually going to be seen by someone intentionally. I was staring at my closet and realizing that almost every shirt I owned was black, every shoe was a type of boot, and every pair of jeans basically looked the same just some had more wear and tear than others. No matter what I picked, I was going to look exactly the same. I settled for a Fleetwood Mac concert tee, some faded holy skinny jeans, and a pair of black combat boots that just so happened to be my favorite. My hair had gotten long, even the part where they put the plate in was growing fast. Mostly because I avoided people, including hairdressers, at all costs. It was almost all the way down to my butt and curly but unruly. I grabbed some leave in conditioner and attempted to tame the curls down to make myself look about ten percent less crazy than I had before. I flipped the part to cover the scar and shorter hair in the spot that the plate was under. Staring at myself in my clothes and with my hair done I realize that I was getting to be a little too thin. My face had hard angles, my shirt dangled loosely even though it was a small, my jeans were being held up by a very sturdy belt and a prayer, and my boots were loose around my calves. I didn't look sick, but I didn't look healthy. I was in an in-between that wouldn't raise any red flags, but nobody would be asking me about any health advice.

I was finally ready to walk out the door at 8:15, and my stomach was doing flips. I hadn't seen him in 6 years. What would he think of me? But the biggest question was, would he think I'd changed too much? Would he notice the spot on my head that I covered with the rest of my crazy hair that hasn't quite grown out yet? Would he notice I had no idea how to act around people in a social setting anymore? Would he notice if I flinched when he moved too fast or came in too close? What if he wanted to hug? Do people even hug anymore? I decided to quit freaking myself out, and grabbed my jacket from the hanger, told Fritz I'd see him soon, and walked out the door and locked it behind me. I made my way down the stairs and out the front door to the lower level and down the street to Don's.

It was a little chilly that night in the breeze. I was standing outside Don's waiting on a familiar face, hoping for the best. Lane came walking up the sidewalk and never missed a beat swinging his arms around me and giving me the biggest and the only hug I've had for a very long time. I didn't know how to react, so I patted him on the back and tried to smile and back away. I felt like I was stiff as a board and I wasn't sure how to really be, but I also just felt at peace for the most part. Seeing Lane, even as awkward as I was, turned out to be like coming home after a long sabbatical. After the awkward hug, he bent in and kissed my cheek and then he reached over and opened the door and waved his arm in a grand gesture to let me enter first, and we went inside to see Don.

Don smiled ear to ear when he saw us actually sit down together and realized that Lane wasn't a stranger that just held the door open for me. Don hadn't met Lane before, or at least not seen him in a very long time and Lane wasn't the type to become best friends with bar owners even if he used to swing by on occasion. Don's was the place everyone knew about, but it wasn't exactly hopping with excitement. It was more of the place you came to when you wanted to escape the excitement and just be with yourself, which I apparently wanted to do more than most. That thought made me feel slightly pathetic again, but I brushed it off. This night was about my friend, not about my insecurities or dwelling on how dysfunctional I was.

We found two seats at the bar in the corner. Don rushed over and asked Lane and I for our order. We both ordered beers and burgers with fries. Don looked at Lane and said, "So you are the friend, huh?" I gave Don a look that would knock lesser men to their knees. Lane laughed and said, "Yes sir, I'm the friend. My name is Lane. I take it you are Don?" Don smiled and reached his hand out to shake Lane's. "In the flesh. I'll put your orders in. The food will be out in a bit." With that, Don reached down in the cooler and grabbed our beers and smiled and winked at me, then chuckled as he walked away. I shook my head, then looked at Lane and smiled bashfully.

He laughed and held his arms up and gave me the once-over look from top to bottom. "You look tiny! Have you lost some weight?" I replied "Yeah, I noticed it today too. Sorry. I don't always eat like I should or sleep like I should, but I'm working on it. You look great! You have basically not changed for the last 6 years." He said, "Yeah, except my eyes. I just can't figure out what is going on with them. The doc I saw said he hadn't seen anything like it but was willing to run some tests. I declined, because tests kind of freak me out and maybe I don't really want to know quite yet what is going on. I just want it to go away. I mean, I can still see, but I can't be in the light hardly at all, so I can't hold a job or do normal daytime things. Mom has been picking up most of the slack and helping me out, but it gets to where I just feel like a burden on her. I've been alone so much that it feels like Mom is basically the only one that speaks to me anymore. I think it weirds everyone else out to see me." Lane was always very social, so being alone for a day relying on his mom to help him would be hard on him, not to mention a longer time. I instantly felt bad for his situation and wanted to help him feel at ease. Don zoomed around the kitchen door and dropped our food off in front of us, grabbed two more beers for us, and winked again and walked away with a huge grin on his face. I rolled my eyes and focused back on Lane.

"Your eyes aren't scary. They just look dark. Do they hurt? Are you having any pain anywhere else with the symptoms?" "No," he started, "it's really just the eyes. But even headlights make my head want to explode. I wear shades almost everywhere; I just didn't want to run up on you with shades on. I was afraid you'd kick my ass." With that, we both laughed. I was always known as one of the guys, and a tough one at that growing up. Three brothers and being raised in the country will make you tough, even if you didn't want to be. I didn't take anything without giving some back, at least until I started dating my ex. Which made the laughing stop on my side rather abruptly. "How are you holding up physically?" he asked. "Well, I have migraines a lot, night terrors, a part time job transcribing online, and Don is the only other human I see on a regular basis. The Doc says I'm improving in some ways, and getting worse in others, and I ran off another Therapist yesterday, but that's just life."

"No, that's not *just life,* D. You can't go through life blaming life on life, mostly because it's not life that did this to you, it was a man. A man that I hope dies a rough death in whatever lockup he is at, but a man, nonetheless. I know you don't want to talk about it, and I know you are still suffering because of it, but I need to say something. Abandoning you when you needed me most was the worst mistake I've made as a friend at any point in life. I should never have done that. You have got to understand that I couldn't watch what he was doing to you and not be able to do something about it. It was the worst feeling. I saw you fading before my eyes every day a little more, and there was absolutely no way of helping you until you wanted help, or he killed you. Thank God, you wanted help after he tried to kill you, but I'm still so very sorry. It shouldn't have gone down that way. I almost lost you forever. When Mom told me the news, I froze, and then I broke down. I wanted to go to the hospital, but figured I'd be the last person you wanted to see." I glared at the floor and wandered if the news had made it to my family, too. I think if it had, one of them would have shown at the hospital, but then again maybe they wouldn't. Maybe those relationships were going to take longer to mend. My family mostly kept to themselves and hated the news or social media, so there was a chance they still didn't know what happened to me a year later, and I was okay with that chance. "Did she tell my parents?" Lane looked up at me and said, "No. She didn't think it was her place to interfere. She had come up to visit me one day and saw the news with his name in the paper and put two and two together. They didn't state your name, so it won't be searchable anywhere by your name either. I don't think they ever found out. I never liked him in school, and I still have no idea how he won you over whenever he did, but that's all in the past. You deserved better from the beginning, but he set his sights on you, and you wouldn't listen to reason from any of us. I know you loved him, D. We just all knew him and his family, and we were all worried we would end up right where we did. We loved you more than he has ever loved anyone."

We both just sat there for a moment with our beers, and I couldn't make eye contact. Not because of the way his eyes looked, but because I knew just how much I had let him down and that he didn't ever really hate me. He just couldn't watch me suffer for years without being able to help me stop the suffering. And then, being the idiot I was, I had walked away from the friendship altogether and not even tried to reach out and see how he was doing. I'd never felt more selfish in my life than I did at that very moment, on that bar stool, sitting beside someone that could have possibly been my friend for the last 6 years, had I not made a lot of the self-destructive choices that I had made. Once again, this all fell on me, and I was finding myself mentally pulling away from the situation to keep myself from falling apart right there in front of everyone.

Finally, I blurted out, "I'm sorry. I know I screwed up. I know the choices I made weren't good or in my best interest, but I can't change them now. I have to try to get past everything and build a life that I can be a participant in, instead of just an observer. I'm trying, Lane. I'm doing my best with the pieces that were left over. He wasn't always bad. Football star, amazing athlete that should have gone places, and he was really sweet to me before we got married. You know he was. You didn't like him, but you didn't hate him back then. You understood why I fell for him. You understood what I wanted, but I know you had a gut feeling, and I should have listened to that, but I'm doing my best now to move forward." "I know, D. I know you are. I see that, but I also see that you are barely functioning at all. Even with my eyes being stupid, I can see that. You aren't happy, you haven't smiled since I hugged you, you are holding on to your beer like it's a life vest, and you keep chewing on your lip, which is cute, but I don't think that's why you are doing it. You are a nervous wreck, and you are keeping something from me, I can tell. So come out with it, what else is going on that has you so on guard constantly?"

"Well, you know how I mentioned the night terrors?" "Yeah. Is that like nightmares?" he asked. "Not exactly. It's like a nightmare that feels so real that you can't decipher that it isn't real. There is no thought that *this is just a dream and I'll wake any minute.* I wake up feeling like I ran a marathon and didn't sleep, rather than having just slept however many hours. I put off sleeping, if possible, on the days that I can. But that's not what I was keeping from you. Last night the night terror was about you." "Did I hurt you?" I was shocked by that question for a minute. Then noticing the true concern on his face, he didn't want him endangering me to be something that my mind would ever come up with. "Yes and no, but not on purpose. You hurt me because you died at the end along with everyone else, and all that was left was an amazing large dog named Duke that appeared to love me until I met the same fate as everyone else."

"I died?" He looked seriously distraught as he asked that question. It was about to get worse. "In the night terror, you had a problem with your eyes. They had gone black. Your face was stuck in a grimace that looked somewhat like a smile, and you were scared. You called me and wanted to see me and asked me for help, but there was nothing I could do for you. Then everyone around started having the same issue, and your eyes started leaking black stuff, and you died." He stared at me like he thought I was playing a cruel joke on him. I looked down and then pushed what was left of my food away. I'd lost my appetite and he was probably going to run for the hills or start yelling at me about how it wasn't a joke that his eyes were messing up and telling me how sick I was for saying what I had. He did none of those things. He just looked at me.

"This happened last night?" He spoke cautiously like he didn't want to know the answer. "Yes, last night or more accurately this morning. I put off sleep till around 5AM. I woke up and just felt off about the entire thing, so I wanted to call you. Almost talked myself out of it but I decided the worst you could do was yell at me or hang up on me, and I probably deserved both of those things, so I quit fighting with myself and just called. Are you mad at me?" He paused a moment then shook his head like he was trying to shake something off. "No, I'm not mad at you. How could I be mad about you telling me the truth? I'm concerned a little. I was thinking about you a lot last night, and I wanted to call you so bad, but I didn't have your number. I *am* scared, my eyes *are* messing up, and I had no idea how to contact the *one* person I wanted to speak to about it. Then today, I get a call from that person, and I'm not sure what that means."

It was my turn to pause a moment. Out of all the people on Earth he could have wanted to contact, he wanted to contact me, and it somehow just so happened that I had a night terror about him in the situation and scared. This was getting a bit crazy. I had missed him more than anyone else, even blood. I also had thought of his name first whenever Don had inquired about friends. I guess I never stopped seeing Lane as a friend, as my best friend, I just didn't know where I stood. I guess I should have known because he apparently felt the same as I did.

"Well, I'm here now, and I have your back. Whatever this is, you will get through it." It was really all I could think of to say. He leaned over and hugged me and just held me there for a long time. Something clicked in my brain, and I remembered *how* to hug, so I hugged him back and laid my head on his shoulder, and we just stayed that way for several minutes. I think we were both needing something from each other, but the biggest thing we needed was just to know the other was there, and for now at least that was good enough for both of us.

The man I married had tortured Lane through school. The whole *bully* thing doesn't really cover it. All the way through grade school and elementary school,

PE was hell for Lane. He was smaller than the other guys and not exactly the most coordinated. He had beat Lane up a couple times, nothing too serious, but serious enough for Lane. He was a couple of years older than us in school, and I still think he is the reason Lane never got into sports in High School. He stayed as far away from that crowd as humanly possible, and I knew that Justin was mostly the reason for that. I should have considered that before I started dating him when I graduated, but a small town, you didn't have a whole lot of people to choose from, so you sometimes had to compromise and settle, which was exactly what I had done. Justin showed interest in me, that's really all he had to do. I didn't stand a chance.

We talked for a few more hours until Don told us he was ready to lock up, but instead of his usual tired and angry face, he was smiling from ear to ear. "Quit smiling so big, Don, or your face will stick like that," I said. He quickly laughed and turned saying "Last call, ya'll finish up and let me sleep. Come back tomorrow if you want and I'll cook you up something special for dinner." I looked at Don like he had lost his mind, because he had never offered me anything but burgers and fries, but I let it slide. He was trying to be nice because I somehow had finally shown up with a friend and he was beaming with pride while looking at me like I was finally becoming something bigger than what my situation had turned me into. I was finally coming out of the funk and taking small steps toward what most people would refer to as *normal.*

# Chapter 3

Lane walked me outside after he refused to let me pay my tab, which was weird for me. "Where are you living now?" He asked while he was standing there with his hands in his pockets looking a bit awkward like he wanted to say something else. "In a loft less than a block down the road," I replied. "Do you want some company on the way home?" He looked nervous, and I wasn't sure why. "Sure, but if you come up, the place is an absolute mess. I don't think I've had a visitor since I moved in. So beware," I warned with a smirk.

We talked as we walked, and then suddenly he stopped walking and turned to look at me. "Can I stay with you tonight? I'd like to make sure you are ok if you have another night terror tonight." I guess that's why he had looked nervous and awkward. He wanted me to be safe, and I get that, but I was dangerous to myself when I slept. I hadn't taken into consideration how dangerous I might be to someone else. Nobody else had ever offered to stay over. "I'd rather you not. Mostly because I don't know what I do during the night terrors. I've bruised myself and even woke up with blood all over me from thrashing in the night. I don't want you to see that or the aftermath. It's not fair to put you or anyone else through my own personal hell. Plus, I'm not sure you would be safe there either." "D, you can't possibly think that I would judge you after all we have been though, and you also can't keep fighting these things alone. Let me be there, maybe subconsciously it will help you and you won't have one tonight, which means best case scenario you actually get a good night's rest, worst case scenario and I see you throwing the fit of a lifetime and just make sure you don't do something you can't take back. Don't worry about my safety, I'll have an advantage. I'll be awake and can hopefully dodge in time."

I continued walking and mulled it over. I figured if I told him no, he would just continue to push it. But, if I told him yes, he would possibly have nightmares of his very own about what he sees during my night terrors. I know I move around a lot and tend to be violent while I have them, but nobody has ever stayed the night before to let me know in the morning how insane I was. Maybe he was right, and maybe it would help. "Ok," I said, "But, you have to promise me that you will still talk to me tomorrow, no matter what happens. Also, don't shake me to wake me up. Doc says it's safer if you just talk to me and try to bring me out of it but do it in a nice and non-threatening tone. Just like you were having a conversation with me and expected an answer. Deal?" "Deal," he replied with a smile. I just hoped he would still smile at me or even be able to look at me tomorrow.

We walked up the stairs, and I let him in. I greeted Fritz and introduced the two of them, and then fed and watered him while ruffling the hair on the top of his head and giving him a kiss. The house wasn't really a wreck because I hated filth. But it was cluttered, and you could tell I lived alone. Mostly alcohol, energy drinks, books, and there was hardly any food to be found seeing as how I usually ate at Don's and hardly ate more than once a day.  I apologized for the mess, like I figured you were supposed to do.  I went to the window to pull the shades closed, because I knew his eyes hurt a lot.  It was dark outside, but there were plenty of lights outside due to us basically being downtown in a city.  I turned on the lamp with the darkest lampshade I had and then I put a sheet over it. Just enough light to where I wouldn't hurt myself walking around, but hopefully not enough to hurt his eyes.

"Thank you," he said, "I didn't mean for you to have to go through extra trouble."  I looked at him and shrugged.  "It's not extra trouble.  I am in pain, and you are staying to make sure that I'm safe through the night.  The least I can do is make sure that I don't cause you pain in the process while I'm awake and can do something about it.  Have a seat, I'll grab us a beer."  I walked to the fridge and opened it and realized not for the first time that it was filled almost full of beer, wine, and cheese.  Again, I don't see anyone coming to me for health advice, but I grabbed the cheese and cubed it, then carried it in on a plate with two open beers in my other hand.  I set his beer and the cheese on the coffee table and leaned back into the couch and took a swig of mine.  "I hate sleeping, Lane.  It could be a while before I'm able to force myself to lay down.  If you need to go ahead and get some rest, you are free to lay down in there.  There is a fold out bed in the couch in my bedroom you can use.  I'll sleep in my bed as soon as I get the courage."  I was trying not to sound as afraid or as awkward as I felt.  "I have a better idea.  Why don't we drink these beers, eat the cheese, and then go lay down and you can lay there while I hold you and

32

hopefully that will help you sleep. You will have the comfort of not being alone before you go to bed. What do you say?" I shrugged and replied, "You do know that I get violent. You could get hurt. If you will stay awake until I drift off, and then move to your own bed, I will feel better. Deal?" "Deal," he said with a smile.

We talked and finished our beers and the cheese, and then made our way into the bedroom. He had seen me change before, so I wasn't too worried, but still asked him to turn around. He obliged and faced the wall while I stripped down and put on shorts and a t-shirt, then offered him some pajama pants and a t-shirt to sleep in. He took them, thanked me, and changed as well while I turned around to give him privacy. We climbed in bed and the last thing I thought before I drifted off was how good and warm he felt, and that he was right. I did feel safe. Maybe tonight will be different.

It was and it wasn't.

### *The Dance*

*It was a little shabby town we had been taken to live in. There was no electricity and the Government had split females into groups and forced them to live together in little huts on one side of town. They gave us stipends to use to get food or smocks to wear, but only if we were able to work for them. The ones that were too old or injured and unable to work got scraps that we portioned out for them from the small stipends we received.*

*I was 39 and living with 8 other women in a two-bedroom hut on West Street. I used to have a husband and a family, but when the Government* decided to take over, we lost all of that. The children were taken to one part of the town, men were taken out of the town to work unless they were Government Employees, and the women were left to do whatever work the Government assigned for the day. Nobody was to interact with anyone else that was from their previous lives.

There was a knock on the door, and I decided I should be the one to answer. All the women in our hut always looked to me for guidance and strength, even though I was scared to death most days, I just chose not to show it. It was my little way of keeping as much control as I could in an uncontrollable situation. Whenever someone knocked, it was never good news. Most of the time they were there to "confiscate" an elderly woman. They did not like that we fed and clothed the women with rations that we received. They wanted us younger and able women to be fed properly and clothed properly so we could perform our duties.

I walked to the door with a sense of dread. When I answered a man dressed in all black with a bitter face was standing there looking down on me. He handed me a letter and said it was not optional and walked away. I stared after him as he jumped up on what they referred to as a "wagon". It was really a beat-up older SUV that they had cut the roof off so the guards could sit in the back and shoot whenever the need occurred. Usually, they didn't shoot at the women. They needed us for picking crops, bailing hay, cleaning, watering plants, making clothes, and other tedious tasks that they would rather not do themselves, but it was still never a good idea to cross them. I'd seen the beatings some women have taken, including myself. I had also seen certain women get shot to death before, just for being disobedient and trying to get others to join them in standing up for themselves. The Government couldn't have us having minds of our own and possibly persuading others to use their minds as well, so they put a stop to it. Abruptly. Every single time.

I took the letter back to our small dining table and the others gathered around, all expecting the worst news. I read the letter aloud so everyone would be able to hear at the same time. "There will be a dance held this Friday for all able-bodied women. You must be dressed in a gown you assemble from rations given to you previously. We will provide one makeup pallet per hut, and you all are to wear this makeup. Anyone who is not wearing the makeup or a dress that looks presentable will face the punishment we see fit. If you are able-bodied and do not attend, you will be punished to the full extent of the law. Be ready for the wagon to pick you up at 6 PM sharp. You will be inspected when we arrive."

We were confused. For a moment, I thought maybe they would bring our husbands back. Just maybe our husbands would be meeting us at this dance. Then, I realized that was a childish dream. They already had the control, why would they give that up? So, my thought process shifted. What was the meaning of this? Why did they need us to show up and who were we supposed to be getting dressed up for? We had so many questions and no answers but a vague letter telling us that if we did not show we would be punished. Several of us had been punished before, again, including myself.

When they first took my husband and children from me, I lashed out. I was so incredibly angry. I broke *one guard's nose and then I stabbed a different guard. I stabbed someone. That was still strange for me to think about. It is humbling to think of what you are capable of when your world gets turned upside-down and you have no choice but to fight. All fighting back had earned me was a bad lashing, two fractured ribs, 12 stitches in my forehead that were crudely done by some guy with bad breath, and some nasty scars himself. I was not pretty to begin with, but now I was way more beaten and broken than when they had taken me.*

*We had two days to throw together dresses and try to remember how to apply makeup. We weren't allowed clocks, so we would need to be ready early just in case we were off on the exact time. Several women wept. I tried to pull everyone together. "We need to get our things together and see what we have on hand to wear or make something out of. Joan, see if you can find us some thread and a needle. Leigh, please see to Meghan and make sure that she is truly unable to attend. We don't want her punished if they think that she is well enough to go. Tracy, please start dinner so we can eat when we have a moment." They all calmed down a bit and saw to their tasks. They looked at me as if I was a mother of sorts, even though I was not the oldest one there. They needed comfort and structure, and I provided that.*

*Comfort and structure. I remember back when I was a wife, and my husband and I had adopted our kids. I gave them comfort and structure. I made sure their days went off without a hitch. I gave everyone their list of things to do and places to be, and then made sure that everyone made it there. Every time I think back to that time, I feel like someone has ripped my heart out of* my chest. I cannot breathe. I cannot move. For just a few moments, I get to remember their faces and what it was like to be a wife and a mother. For just a moment, I'm not in this hell with these people in charge of us that have to be a special kind of sick in the head to do the things they do to people.

We had three elders in the hut. Most huts only took in one elder, but I couldn't bear to think of these beautiful women living to their 70s and beyond and then being reduced to sleeping outside in the elements and eating burned scraps that have been thrown into dumpsters. Not while I was alive. I wouldn't stand for it. Our elders were special to my heart and Morgan, Genevieve, and Grace were their names. Grace was about 85 and a beautiful soul. Genevieve was 72 and reminded me of Dorothy off the Golden Girls. She seemed like she would have been a spitfire in her day and had an opinion about everything, though she was careful not to share that opinion except to us girls. Morgan never spoke. She was the oldest, but we never did know exactly how old she was, though she looked to be in her 90's. I'm not sure if she had nothing to say, or if she had just mentally checked out to save herself from having to deal with what the rest of us faced daily. They would not be attending and could barely stand these days, so they were tasked with just staying alive, if possible, in hopes that we could someday be free, and they would see their families or get proper medical treatment for the ailments that creeped in on them in their old age.

I walked onto the back closed-in porch by candlelight and looked at our smocks. We had 15 smocks between us all, and none of them very pretty.

Most seemed to be made from old pillowcases that someone had thrown together to make sure that we never forgot our low status among everyone else in this town. We had 8 women, so several would have to wear the same smock today and tomorrow to be able to get some of the smocks to look better before we had to leave for the dance. Joan came back with the needle and thread, and I started working on sinching the waist of a few of the smocks and using Joan as a model. We were all about the same size due to being starved and rationing out our food to the three elders. I cut the bottom of the smock off that was ratted and torn and made a belt and bow for around the waist where I had sinched them. I got three smocks done, and I knew it was getting late, but I wanted to make sure I'd be able to have five finished in time, so I went back to look and see if I could find two others that weren't in terrible shape.

I found the two that were most put together and started to work on them. I needed fabric to patch them, and did not have any scraps, so I had to sacrifice another smock to make the patches. By the time I had finished the dresses, it had been dark for an awfully long time. I wasn't sure of the exact time, but I knew that daylight would come early tomorrow, and we were forced to be up at daylight to work. Joan said she would be sure that she woke me up as soon as she got up in the morning, so I thanked her, and I went to bed. I laid there wondering what the dance would bring. Would we be held as slaves to new captors and split from our elders that we cared for? Would I ever see Joan and the others after that fateful night? Would I even be alive after that night? I struggled to sleep and didn't feel like I had gotten any rest when Joan came in the next morning to wake me and make sure I was up and getting ready for the day.

The next day felt like a death sentence. We all felt that somehow this dance would be the end of us. Maybe they were luring us all there to kill us and be done with it. Maybe they were going to pair us off with the lonely Government Employees and we would be forced to take on new roles in their houses. The last possibility scared us all the most. We had not been subjected to living with other males, but that did not mean that they couldn't change their minds and auction us off like cattle. What would I do if they paired me with someone? How would I manage to get myself through that? It seemed unbearable to me to live with any other man than the man that I vowed to love forever and find my way back to. The man that had held me up through everything and gave me a strength that I had to pull from these days, even though he was nowhere to be seen. I used him for strength daily. I was going to see him again, and I would not give myself to another man in any fashion without a fight. In this instance, that fight would most likely end in my death, but these days death seemed a better option most of the time.

None of us could sleep that night. We were too scared of what was to come the next day. At dawn, a man showed up with water and told us to come outside so he could spray us off. We were not to work today, but to focus on getting prepared for the evening activities. We were forced to undress and stand by the side of the hut while he sprayed us with a power washer and made us scrub down with powder detergent. We weren't given anything with which to dry ourselves off on and had no extra smocks to use for the task, so we all just stood there dripping and trying to keep ourselves covered until we knew it was safe and we were dry enough to step inside the house. He took a tiny pallet of makeup to the doorstep and put it at the base of the door. He looked us over with a grimace and scoffed as he turned and left us there naked, degraded, and scared to death of what was going to come of us later that evening.

We went inside and started to assemble outfits together. We did not have shoes and were never provided any, so barefoot would have to do. The makeup pallet had base, blush, powder, eyeshadow, and lipstick all in extremely small quantities that would have to be rationed to be sure we all had enough on to pass inspection. Meghan took turns putting makeup on us, while forcing herself to stand as much as possible. They had broken both of her legs when she tried to run after her family as they were dragged away from her. The town doctor they took her to had put makeshift braces on her legs after the incident and left them as they were to set gnarled and crooked, but we were all afraid they would punish her if she did not attend, so she forced herself to stand through the pain to try to prepare herself mentally for the night ahead.

We all looked as "pretty" as we were going to get, so we waited. The wagon pulled up and several men unloaded and began the inspections. They made us stand side by side and scrutinized every detail that we had worked so hard to make as decent as humanly possible. Meghan was seen unfit to attend because of her legs, so she was sent back inside. In that moment, we all envied her. They lined us up in single-file and pushed us up into the wagon. Tracy and Leigh had to sit on Joan and my laps so the guards could have their own place to sit. The wagon took off and we all ignored the aching in our bodies and our hearts as it was too late to run now. There was no place to run to even if we had been given the opportunity and took it.

We arrived at a massive plantation house that had cattle and horses, neither of which we had seen in years. Cattle and horses were a luxury, though I'm not sure who they had to care for them. I'm sure that they didn't care for them on their own. We exited the wagon and were escorted inside the main entrance where a group of men were standing and staring at us. By the looks on their faces, it didn't seem that any of them had seen a woman in some time. Immediately, my stomach began to turn. In the line of men, I searched desperately for my husband. I had no luck in finding him. The stares bore into me and I could feel my face heating up. This wasn't going to happen. I wasn't going to let them pair me off with a stranger. I wouldn't go down without a fight. I couldn't.

They began to pair us off and our new escorts took us to a table where they had fine dishes and glassware. It was almost like I had been transplanted into an old movie set, except I was highly underdressed, angry, and terrified. The men that we were paired with never spoke a word to us and as usual, it was implied that we were not to speak unless spoked to. We ate in silence when the food was served and then we were escorted to the dance floor with our dance partners.

I had never learned to properly dance, so I was clumsy. It was only about 15 seconds into the first song when I stepped on my partners foot and immediately found myself on the ground. It was a moment or two *before I realized he had backhanded me, and I found my legs too weak to stand up and when I reached up to feel my face, my hand came back smeared with my own blood. He glared down at me and reached down and backhanded me the other direction and knocked my head back down into the floor. It felt like my jaw was dislocated. He walked closer to me and kicked me in the stomach and reared back to kick me again, but before his foot collided a streak of fabric passed over me and the man froze as Joan stood in front of him. It took me a minute to clear my eyes from tears to see that there was blood flowing down from several holes in the man's chest. Joan had taken a knife from one of the tables that hadn't been cleared and stabbed him at least 6 times before he fell to the ground right beside where I lay.*

*She helped me up and we stood together while the guards started rushing towards us. It was like every woman in the room saw that as a time to go into action. They all immediately reached for whatever could be used as a weapon. I grabbed a vase off a shelf that was made of metal, and we rushed the guards. There was a lot of blood, women and guards falling, escorts falling, but at the end of it, there were several of us women still standing. We ran. We ran as fast and as far as we could without ever looking back to see if we were being followed.*

*We were still running when we spotted a stream. Joan and I were the only two out of our hut that were able to get out of the plantation. The rest of the women were from other huts. I'm not sure if the others survived or sacrificed themselves for our freedom, but I wasn't going back to find out. We* stopped at the stream to get a drink and kept running. We came upon a fence that was made of stone and helped each other over it. About a mile or so down the road, we noticed a house sitting off to the side with cattle, horses, pigs, and some goats. We stopped to stake it out. Joan went up to a window and saw a man, woman, and three children about to sit down for dinner.

I knocked on the door while the others hid around the side of the house. The woman answered the door and asked what my business was there. I told her what had happened and asked where we were. She immediately told me to gather my friends and get inside. She called the police, which scared me at first as we were told that was who had taken us. The police showed up and explained that there was a terrorist group that had overtaken parts of the city and we were victims of this attack. Our husbands had been rescued a while back and were safe and awaiting our return. They asked our names and our old addresses and got to work searching for our families.

About four hours passed by as we sat there listening to everything the officers were telling us about how life had changed these years we had been gone. They dubbed us heroes for our acts of savagery against the men that were most likely going to attempt to make us their own. They gathered an army of men to overtake the compound after we pointed them in the right direction.

I stayed silent. We hadn't run but a few miles. Why hadn't they searched harder for us? Why did it take them years to rescue us? Where were my family members? How many died agonizing deaths at the hands of those men?

*I looked out the front window to see my husband's face staring back at me. He had our children tucked up under his arms and looked like he was afraid of me being angry with him. I cautiously went to the door and walked out into the air. I walked to the edge of the porch, and then I couldn't walk any more. I fell to my knees and my children rushed over and hugged me, held me, stroked my hair, climbed in my lap, and we all cried. My husband slowly walked forward and knelt beside me and took my hand in his hand. "I will never let anyone hurt you ever again, as long as I live. Do you believe me?" I nodded, mostly because I was afraid words wouldn't form and the only thing that would come out of my mouth was a deafening sob. He sat down and pulled me and the kids into his lap, and we stayed like that on the porch for hours. Nobody tried to hurry us and nobody tried to intervene. We were together again and in that moment, I couldn't have asked for anything better.*

# Chapter 4

I woke with a start, and realized I smelled bacon cooking. My head started to clear from the fog, and I looked over and realized I had forgotten Lane had stayed. I looked down and had several new yellow-purple welts on my legs and arms and probably one of my eyes too from the pain when I felt of it. It hadn't worked, or had it? I still had the night terror, but it had a somewhat happy ending. Happy enough for me to have woken up and not thrown up or had a migraine. I had fought, I had won, and I had saved people in the process. I had gotten my "husband" back even though I have no idea who the man's face belonged to that had stared back at me in the dream.

I whistled for Fritz, like an all clear when I woke up, and he came in and hopped into my lap and gave me kisses. I'm not sure how that dog knew that I was *safe* after my eyes opened, but he never tried to join me in the bed while I was sleeping. At least not to my knowledge. I got myself up and went ahead and threw on pants and a long-sleeved shirt, mostly to hide the evidence of last night, and I walked into the kitchenette and saw Lane's back as he was standing at the stove. He turned around and I froze. My breath caught in my throat, and I almost started crying right then and there. The left side of his face was swollen up terribly and his eye was blood red in the very little visible part that should have been white, like the vessels had burst in it. He had full on handprints on his right arm and bruises down his left leg. Before he could open his mouth, I ran to the bathroom and threw up in the toilet, and I lost it. I sobbed and couldn't catch my breath. The next minute Lane was in the floor with me, cradling me on his chest between his legs, and just letting me sob. When I had calmed down to a point where I could hear him talk, he said, "Hey, listen to me, D, it wasn't your fault. I fell asleep and forgot to move over. When I woke up, you were in deep and I was scared to move, and then when I did move, I think I made it worse. You followed me, but it wasn't your fault. It wasn't you. You didn't know. Calm down. I'm absolutely fine. I got

45

beat up worse than this in school on a regular basis, remember? Please calm down and quit crying. I know you would never do this to me on purpose. Breathe, D."

I looked up at him, but I didn't say anything. Words wouldn't form and neither would thoughts. He said, "Get your butt in the living room, and sit on the couch. I made coffee and a huge breakfast to give you some calories back from what you burned throughout the night. I think I realized why you are so tiny now. You basically ran the equivalent of a marathon and performed 3 boxing matches. You need food, now go." I got up and made my way blankly to the couch and sat down and stared. The curtains had kept the sun out for the most part, so I guess I had that to be thankful for. I beat him up, but at least his eyes won't add to the pain on my account. He brought over a plate with two fried eggs over medium like I like them, toast with butter and jelly, and a bunch of bacon. I guess he figured my tastes hadn't changed that much in 6 years, and they hadn't. He went back to the kitchen and came back with a huge cup of coffee made black with sugar, exactly how I liked it. The mug must have been newly bought, because I didn't have one that big in the loft, but I didn't ask him. He even had scrambled an egg and put it on top of Fritz's bowl, which was keeping him occupied at that moment.

Lane brought his own plate in there and sat down and started eating like nothing had happened. I just stared at him for a minute. "I can't believe that I did that to you. Sorry doesn't even cover what I'm feeling. You can't stay here again, ever." He looked at me like I'd just slapped him on the bruised side of his face. "Like hell, I can't. You don't scare me, and like I said, it was my mistake. It won't happen again. Now that I know what I'm dealing with I'm definitely not leaving you here to deal with it all on your own. Not happening. Not now, and not in the future until we can get you lined out where you stop hurting yourself all night long," he stated matter of fact like. Then he went back to eating, again like nothing had happened.

I didn't know what to do or how to react. Then he looked over at me and made a face and gestured to my plate like if I didn't start eating, I would be in trouble. So, I ate. I figured the least I could do was eat the breakfast he had gone out and bought, hopefully before daylight, and cooked for me. It was delicious. The boy always knew how to cook great food. He learned well from his Momma. After I finished, I grabbed my plate and his too, and I took off to the kitchen to wash them. I decided I didn't feel like washing by hand, so just rinsed them, put them in the dishwasher, and went ahead and ran it. I never used the dishwasher usually, because being just me there, it took me forever to have enough dishes to fill the thing up. By the time I could fill it up, there wasn't a dish in the house. That probably explains why Lane decided to pick some dishes up while he was out this morning.

"Why are you being so kind to me? I see you for the first time in 6 years and beat you up within 24 hours of seeing you. I warned you that this was a bad idea and you insisted anyways. You are welcome to stay here, but I have to go see Dr. Baker today. I pissed off another therapist, and she left me a voicemail that I had an appointment at 2 PM." "Why don't I go with you?" he asked. "No way. She will know that I did that

47

to you. She will go into a ton of details about why you should stay as far away from me as possible, which I've already told you, but she will be more imaginative in how she will tell you. Dr. Baker likes me enough, I guess, but she doesn't think I'm a good prospect for anyone to be around, and most of the time I agree with her. Plus, you can't be out in the daylight." He looked at me like that was the dumbest statement I'd said all morning. "I won't melt, D. I'm going. I don't think she is doing enough for you. And apparently therapy isn't going to work if you keep scaring off the therapists, so maybe she has an idea of what I can do to help. I'm going. Bottom line." I smirked a little and looked up at his poor face. "You are bossy, you know that? I've been on my own an entire year, and you come out of nowhere and I'm taking orders from you. Fine. You can go. But only because I still feel guilty, which I'm sure you will use as long as you can." "Damn right I will," he said with a snicker. "Whatever," I said, "get dressed."

He was still smiling, though it was a little lopsided due to the bruising, as he got up and went to the bedroom to change back into his clothes from the day before. I just sat there, still in shock from what had happened, until I realized time was getting short and I needed to go brush my teeth and at least try to look alive for the appointment. I splashed water on my face, brushed my teeth, and put the bare minimum makeup on then opened the door to leave the bathroom. Lane grabbed me as I was coming out of the bathroom and pulled me into another of his deep hugs and I laid my head on his shoulder and he leaned into my ear and said, "Breathe. I'm fine and I'm going to make sure that you are fine as well before I leave you. That's all." He let go and a tear slid down my cheek, and I batted it away as quickly as possible. He grabbed my hand, threaded it through his arm, we both said goodbye and gave kisses to Fritz, and then he walked me out the door. At the bottom of the stairs he asked which way, and I veered him left toward Dr. Baker's office.

When we arrived, I signed in like normal, but the desk clerk looked like she was about to have a stroke. I'm not sure if it was the sight of Lane or just the fact that I actually had someone with me that surprised her, but she was definitely surprised. Dr Baker called my name from her office, which is her usual, and I walked to the door and opened the door wider and Lane and I stepped inside. She looked up and her eyes got huge. "Hello, please have a seat. Delaney, who might this be and what happened to his face?" She said it nicely, but still accusatory. "Hey Doc, this is Lane. A childhood friend. He stayed the night last night and didn't take my advice to move to the separate bed and was at the receiving end of my night terror last night. I don't think he will hesitate to take the separate bed going forward." She grimaced and pointed to his lap where his hands were laying. "Lane, show me your arms, please." Lane pulled up his sleeves and showed her the bruises. "Do your legs look about the same?" she asked. "Yeah, but I'm fine. It wasn't her at all, it was like she was someone else entirely. I just wanted to help." He was nervous. I had no idea why he was nervous with *my* doctor, but he acted like he was on trial.

Doc continued her ritual with me. "Roll up your sleeves please, Delaney." I complied. "Do your legs look about the same as your usual?" she asked. "Yes ma'am, they do." "Did you write down the plot?" she

49

inquired. "Yes ma'am. I've been writing them down since I saw you a couple days ago." She nodded like I had completed an assignment on time and therefore at least did that part right. "Did you tell Mr. Lane here about the night terror?" I shook my head and said, "No ma'am, not this one in particular." She still had the same expression on her face, giving nothing away when she asked, "Why not?" I shrugged and replied, "Because this one didn't have him in it." It was my honest answer, and she knew it. Dr. Baker is one of the few people on Earth that I respect and trust. Lane wouldn't know that, of course, but I think he was getting the sense that she was special to me, and I to her. She turned her attention back to Lane. "Lane, did you wake her up?" "No ma'am," he said using the same tone as I had, "I tried what she said you had told her, you know, to speak to her in a calm voice like I needed her to answer me without touching her." This time she nodded and looked like Lane completed an assignment on time and done it in a satisfactory manner. "I take it that didn't work." Lane shook his head. "No ma'am, that didn't work. She panicked and that's when I got the shot to the eye." I flinched. I didn't like hearing his side of what had happened. I hated that I had hurt him, and the fact that I had hurt him within a day of seeing him after 6 years added insult to injury, literally. "Delaney, did you bring your journal as I asked?" I nodded. "Yes ma'am, here it is." I reached over and handed her the journal I had bought for the night terrors. It was leather and plain with a sewn-in bookmark. She opened it and began to read.

She didn't look back up until she had finished both terrors, and I couldn't read her expression, but to me, she looked sad. I hadn't re-read them since I wrote them.  That wasn't part of the assignment.  She just said to write them down so hopefully it would assist me in moving on, but she had mentioned nothing of reading them, and I wasn't going to volunteer.  When she looked back up, she looked extremely pensive, like something had stuck out to her.  "Lane, I can see you actually are having issues with your eyes.  Did this happen before the terror?  Or after?"  Lane looked up and replied, "My eyes have been like this for a while, but progressively getting worse.  Delaney didn't know about my eye issue until the day after she had the terror.  She called because she just had a sense that I needed someone, or I needed help and because Don had given her grief about not attempting to have friends.  And I'm glad she did call because I was struggling.  So technically, it predates the terror, but doesn't predate the terror where Delaney is concerned.  She found out after it."  Dr. Baker nodded.  "When was the last time you two had spoken before this terror?"  "Six years ago," Lane said rather sadly.  His entire face kind of sank like he was regretting it.

Dr. Baker took the hint and didn't pry.  "Delaney, these are very vivid and very scary, but very different as well.  Usually with night terrors, they have a common ground or a common issue.  The only commonality I can find is it's you against the world.  That isn't a safe mindset for someone in your condition.  The fact that Lane was there and was supporting you, and you still had a terror bad enough to where you caused him bodily harm, which I'm sure you feel terrible about, means that these are deeply rooted.  These fears and circumstances are something you truly feel, but then your imagination takes them to another level.  I know what happened with the therapist.  I should have known better than to send you to her, knowing how both of you are, it wasn't a good fit. I take full responsibility for that. But I truly think something has got to give and you need help with the side of it that isn't physical, and I am not equipped to give that to you, even if I *am* the only person you like in my field. I want to try a different approach. I want you to meet a new person every day. Like really meet, not just see them. I want you to walk up, introduce yourself, find something in common or something you can speak about for a moment, and then write it up. Every day. You have been on the sidelines too long watching the world pass you by, and you have got to stop feeling so isolated. If you won't do therapy, this is an option to bring you out of the *me versus them* mentality, and have you start seeing people as people instead of as opponents. Do you think you can do that for me?"

I stared. I wasn't sure I could do what she was asking, but I knew her enough and respected her enough that I wanted to try. "Okay Doc, I'll try. If I happen to miss a day, can I just pick up the next day?" She smiled. "Of course," she said, "but focus on not missing a day. One person a day isn't a lot to ask for, and there are no stipulations. A clerk at a store, a homeless person with nothing better to do than talk, a smoker on the street, or a police officer are all viable options. Just speak to them, get their name, and what you talked about and write it down in your night terror journal, and please bring it to your next appointment. I'm going to have Maggie go ahead and set an appt for 2 o'clock next week on Tuesday. Try to get Tuesday's person met before you show up that day, please. You can do this Delaney, please do your best." She said the last part with finality, like there was no room for error even though she had given me a little grace in person. "Yes ma'am. I will do what I can."

She turned to Lane. "I would like to know what medications you are on." Lane looked puzzled, but replied, "I take an antidepressant and some multivitamins, but that's about it." She nodded and said she would like to do some bloodwork if it was okay. Lane shrugged and said it was fine, so Dr. Baker had a nurse come in to take Lane's blood. She looked at him and said "If you are going to be taking care of Delaney, we need to make sure we can get you fixed up, if possible, as well. I'll run some tests and get back to you. Hopefully we can get your eyes lined back out to where you don't have the dilation issue. Will you be joining us next week?" she asked a little pointedly. I think she liked that he was watching over me. "Yes ma'am, I'll be here," Lane replied with a side glance in my direction. I didn't look back. I felt like I was being cornered and told to break down all the barriers that had kept me somewhat safe and somewhat sane this year, but I knew them both. They both meant well, even if this was going to be a rough week. Maybe I could keep from sleeping tonight and only deal with it tomorrow night. Something in the back of my mind told me that Lane wasn't going to let me skip nights of sleep, though. Regardless of how hard I pushed; he would want me to rest. I do think he will choose not to lay with me in the same bed moving forward, which made me feel better and broke my heart all at the same time.

Dr. Baker looked at us and said, "I will see you both next week. Thank you for making it today." And with that, we were dismissed. It was almost 3 o'clock and that's my usual time to go to Don's and have a burger and fries or at least fries. Maybe there would be someone inside Don's I could meet. We walked out of the office and onto the sidewalk. "You want to go to Don's and get some fries and a beer with me?" I asked Lane. "Sure, but first, I want you to walk over there to that girl and ask her name and introduce yourself," he said with a smirk. "Lane, that girl is a prostitute. I'm pretty sure they get into trouble for speaking without money changing hands." In all fairness, I wasn't sure she was a prostitute, but she was on a corner downtown with very little clothes on, so one could guess. "I don't see anyone watching her, and she looks pretty lonely. It's 3 in the afternoon. If a car pulls up just wave and leave her be but go at least introduce yourself." I wasn't having it. "Aren't I supposed to have something in common with who I speak with?" Lane giggled and said, "No. You are supposed to *find* something in common with who you speak with." I rolled my eyes, already annoyed with the break in my routine, which made Lane laugh even harder even though his face was swollen, and it probably hurt. I looked like a disgruntled teenager.

I took off walking to the girl, and she saw me approaching almost as soon as I set out in her direction. She looked like she was a little concerned but seemed to reach the conclusion that I wasn't a threat, so she said nothing until I got close enough to speak to her. "Hey, I'm Delaney. I really like your boots. Where did you get them from?" Her face snarled up and she glared at me. "They're mine. I didn't steal them if that's what you're asking. Who the hell do you think you are?" That startled me. So much for these people not being opponents. "I never thought you stole them, I'm sorry. I think you misunderstood me." She

54

interrupted, "What? Do you think I'm too stupid to understand plain English? You are over here snooping around where you have no business, why don't you turn around and go back to the dude with the black eye over there."

I paused a beat. I was losing hope that this would turn into a positive experience, but when in doubt, the truth usually beats all. At least it will be a conversation I can write down. I looked her in the eyes and said, "You are tough, and I get that. I respect that. I wish I had been tougher in my life, and maybe I wouldn't have gotten my skull cracked open by my ex and left on the side of the road to die. Maybe I wouldn't fear everyone I meet and getting close to anyone just in case they might be the next person to hurt me. Maybe things would have been different for me if I had been tough like you, but I wasn't tough. Now my doctor tells me I need to realize the entire world isn't out to get me by going up and speaking to random strangers and introducing myself, and my only friend in the world, the one you called the dude with the black eye, is over there trying to be supportive and pointed you out as the first person. I'm sorry I interrupted your life, and I do hope that your toughness takes you places in life that I will never get to go."

With that, I turned to walk away, but she said "Wait. Are you Delaney Jameson? The girl that almost died a year ago? Your name wasn't in the paper, but it was all over town what happened to you. I felt so bad for your situation, love, but being tough wouldn't have saved you. Nothing short of a bullet to that guy's head would have saved you. Nobody thinks you are less of a person because of it, and nobody is out to get you. The boots were given to me by a girl I worked with before she killed herself. I'm sorry I was snappy with you; I just have had a few hard months myself." I turned to face her. "It's fine. Turns out talking to strangers isn't one of my strengths. Thank you for speaking to me though, and I'm around here a lot, and tend to veer towards Don's on a normal basis. If you ever need anything, just come find me, okay? Take care of yourself." She called, "Hey, wait! Don't you want to know my name at least?" "Sure," I said. She smiled and said, "Meagan. Maybe I'll see you around at Don's. It was nice to meet you, Delaney." I returned the smile. "Nice to meet you too. Stay safe," and with that I walked back to Lane with the biggest smile on my face staring at the biggest lopsided smile on his. He said, "I figured it would either become a fight or a friendship, turns out it was both. Let's go get a beer." We walked toward the entrance of Don's with my hand looped through his arm. He opened the door to Don's again for me with the same grand gesture with his arm allowing me to go in before him. I stepped in out of the sidewalk, still smiling from my tiny accomplishment.

## Chapter 5

Don's was pretty empty and Don was smiling ear to ear at the sight of us. I knew he knew what happened to Lane's face, at least he could make a great guess. He didn't waver, though. He waved us over to the bar. "Come on in and have a seat at the bar. I went and picked some special stuff up for you all to eat. Give me just a bit and I'll whip it up for you. Tend to the bar while I'm gone if anyone comes in, will you Delaney?" I smiled at him and silently thanked him for not mentioning Lane's face. "Sure, Don. Thanks."

"He is so adorably weird," I said as I turned to Lane who was just sitting there looking at me and grinning that lopsided grin. I'd almost become used to the black eye and bruises at that point. They didn't bother me quite as much as they had before, even though I had been the one to cause the damage. That part still made my stomach sink. "He cares about you, D. I think he sees himself as somewhat of a father-figure to you and he feels responsible for you. Let him have this. It's making him happy to see you around someone else. He doesn't have to worry about you being alone all the time. Though I do find it weird that he didn't mention my eye."

"He knows about the terrors, Lane. I told him one night after I'd had a few too many. I told him how dangerous I was to myself when I had them. He probably put two and two together and realized that I was also a danger to others, and you had stayed the night with me. He is probably just happy that you stuck around through it, and even though I apparently hurt you, you didn't hurt me back. Instead, like a nut, you made me breakfast and went to my doctor's appointment with me. Some would say that *you* were the one with issues." I smiled and turned to face him. "Good one. I just know you. I know you are a great person with a huge heart. I saw your reaction when you saw my face. You would never intentionally hurt me, and that's all I need to know to be just fine. I also would never intentionally hurt you, which you know, so you are going to be just fine. It's an adjustment, not a burden."

I didn't really know what to say at that point, so I went around the counter and brought us out a couple of beers. I put the coasters down so Don wouldn't get snippy with me and snap out of his cheerful mood, even though the bar itself had seen better years. We sat there in silence for a minute, and then Lane looked at me with caution on his face and said, "D, why haven't you spoken to your parents? Why haven't you let them be around and help? They were always around when we were younger." I looked down and took a drink of my beer before I answered. "Honestly? It's my fault. My parents didn't approve of my ex, so I pulled farther and farther away from them. Basically, I did the same with them that I did with you. I haven't spoken to them since the wedding. I'm not sure how to even approach them these days. They are back home, I'm sure, still the same as they've always been. But I'm not the same, Lane. I've changed so much; I don't think they would recognize me. Either the news didn't make it all the way home about the accident, they didn't care enough to show up, or they figured I didn't want them there to rub it in my face that they were right all along. I just can't face them. Not yet, not until I know how I'm going to fix myself and get back to a resemblance of the daughter they once knew. They deserve that much, or maybe I'm just too scared to face them at all. I'm not sure." I quit talking and picked up the beer and took a long pull off it. I sat it down and hung my head.

Lane reached over and put his fingers underneath my chin and lifted my head and shifted it towards him. "Your parents talk to my mom regularly. They have no idea where you are at or what's become of you. They have no idea if you are still alive or if he killed you years ago and they never got to bury their daughter. They worry all the time but have nothing to go off of because Mom doesn't want to get involved where she doesn't belong, and honestly, we only knew about the accident, not much else. They hired a private investigator at one point that took all their savings but gave them little to no results. Just a picture of you walking to the store one day. That's all. One picture, D. But they kept it and they cherish it, and they show it to anyone who will look at it. They never stopped loving you, and they never stopped caring. They just didn't have the resources to find a woman that didn't want to be found. And you made it impossible for anyone to find you, even me. I tried several times as well. You live, work, eat, go to the doctor, and shop on a 3-block radius in a city filled with hundreds of thousands of people. The odds of anyone just happening on that 3-block radius is slim to none. Especially if they have no idea what they are looking for. You are half the size you used to be, and your hair is twice as long, but in your defense, you still dress the same." He said that with a snicker, and I slugged him playfully in the arm.

"Let me get myself together. Let me work on me a little more with your help. Then I'll think about calling them, deal?" I loved my family, but I just wasn't quite ready for all the questions and awkwardness yet. "Deal. Now I need another beer, barmaid." I rolled my eyes and smiled. I knew he was trying to lighten the mood. "Shut up Lane, but okay. Just a second." As I got up to go around the bar to grab us another beer, the door opened, and someone came inside. The light from outside was shading their face, so I couldn't see who it was. I squinted and said, "Have a seat anywhere you want. What would you like to drink?" A deep, timid voice answered me. "Whatever is cold will do fine, thank you." I nodded and went to the cooler. "No problem. Coming right up."

The light settled and the door closed, and I turned around and saw his face. It was my ex-husband Justin's big brother Joe. Once upon a time, that man had been the only kind thing in my life. He knew about the abuse, and he would bring me things like bandages or new sunglasses or ointment depending on what had happened so I didn't have to go outside where people could see me. After what happened I had really hoped I would never see anyone in that family again, regardless of whether they had showed kindness or not. Why would he come here? What did he want? I realized at that point that I had frozen, and Lane was watching me very carefully and looking at the guy out of the corner of his good eye.

"Hey D. Did Don hire you on?" I still just stood there. Beer in hand and frozen in time. What was going on? Why had he shown up here? What was I supposed to do? The first thing I wanted to do was run, but I had nowhere to run to. Joe put his hands up in a gesture that was universally understood that the person meant no harm, and said, "I just came to tell you something I thought you should know." He made his way to the bar. I handed over the beer, and still stood there silent. Don had come out of the kitchen and stood in the doorway and was watching to make sure I was okay. I guess you *can* hear silence and tension. Don said, "Now Joe, we talked about this. What are you doing here, son?" I hadn't seen Joe since he followed me to Don's after Justin was arrested. Don had laid down the law immediately, and he knew that he wasn't welcome. That had been almost a year ago to the day. "I just need a minute with Delaney, and then I'll leave. Promise, Don. I'll even pay for the beer. Delaney can I just speak to you for a minute? Is that okay?" I shrugged because I still couldn't find any words and gestured towards a booth in the back. We both went and sat there silent for a moment, and then he started in on the news.

"Hey kid, something came up in the case. I know they said you wouldn't have to testify, and I don't want you to have to testify, but they are about to get a lot of evidence thrown out on a technicality. I loved you liked a sister, and you know that, and the last thing I want is him back out on the streets because some file clerk messed up somewhere." Joe was always riding the fence. He never took either of our sides, so I was confused as to why he was here instead of talking to the defense attorney for his brother. "What evidence are they throwing out?" He looked at me hard and said, "They are trying to throw out all the medical records, especially the ones from the accident." My face turned red and I couldn't stop myself. "Can you stop calling it a damn accident, for the life of me I never could imagine how throwing someone from a car on a highway on her head could be construed as an *accident*. It was no accident. He wanted me dead, and he almost got his wish. How the hell can they toss that evidence out?" He looked down apologetically and said, "The file clerk apparently misfiled it. They went to get it for court, and it wasn't there. They can get it all again from the hospital records, but the defense is fighting that it could be tainted since it has been a year and it was such a high-profile situation." "Evidence like that doesn't get *misfiled,* Joe. The evidence didn't walk off. Someone took the evidence. So, what you are saying is that he gets to walk. That's all the evidence. The other times, I didn't tell them it was him that did it to me in the ER. They would paint me as a bad witness, a liar, delusional, or basically whatever they wanted. Which also means my testimony is no good either, Joe. Who is going to listen? And there is no way I can face him in court." He nodded, "I spoke to the Prosecutor. You wouldn't have to face him, just his lawyer. You would have a one-on-one interview with both the Prosecutor and the Defense Attorney, and then the Judge would make the decision on whether the evidence can stay in for Trial or not. I also agreed to testify as a witness for the Prosecution. I saw more than my fair share of times that he abused you, D. You deserved better from the beginning, and I told him that time and time again. With you, he just saw red."

There it was, the *with you* part. His entire family had played it off like I was something that he just couldn't handle. I wasn't technically the problem, but I was the cause of the problem, whether I wanted to be or not. I couldn't leave, he wouldn't let me. But staying made him crazier, and so what exactly was I supposed to do with that? How was I supposed to fix him? The man was nothing but evil and will ever only be evil. There was no fixing him. There was also no trusting anyone in that family. I took what Joe said with a grain of salt, but not to be true. I was skeptical in the least.

"Joe, I think you should leave. Now, please. Tell the Prosecutor if he absolutely needs me that he can find me through Don. I'm not giving *you* my number. Please don't ever come looking for me again." I was shaking. I was hurt, but also scared, and I couldn't put a finger on why. I know Justin was still in jail awaiting trial. I knew they hadn't thrown away the key to his cell yet, but I had also figured it was an open and shut case. It was in the back of my mind, not the front. I didn't have to deal with it. I was told I wouldn't ever have to deal with it again. I was lied to, and I hate being lied to. At this point, I wasn't sure if Joe was lying to my face as well, so I was trying to remain calm until there was a reason for me to react.

Joe got up, head down, and made his way to the door. He turned around before he exited and said, "Delaney, I'll do what I can do to prevent this, okay? I'm trying. Don, I'm sorry I interrupted your evening. Ya'll have a great night." With that he walked out and left me still sitting in the back corner booth stunned. Tears just started streaming down my face. There wasn't anything I could do to stop them. Lane got up, picked up both of our beers, came over and sat on the booth next to me and put the beers on the table. He leaned over and pulled me into his chest. He had probably heard everything as Don's wasn't the best place for a private conversation. I wasn't 20 feet from the bar at the farthest corner.

"What am I going to do, Lane?" I asked as I looked up at him. "This particular fight was supposed to be over a long time ago. I can't face him, and I won't face him. I should never have to see his face again, not after what I went through. Even if I don't have to see

63

him while I'm testifying, he will be there, in that building, sitting in the courtroom, or around a corner somewhere, but he will be there. And even that depends on if Joe is telling the truth, which I'm not sure he is. If he is, someone took that evidence, Lane." Lane hugged me tighter. "D, he is just a man. He can't hurt you surrounded by guards and people in public, so there is no way he could do anything to you even if you do have to show up to speak on your own behalf. I will find 7 guys to stand around you where he can't even lay eyes on you if you want. I'll do whatever it takes if it comes down to you having to face this again, but hopefully his brother is being real with you, and he will actually try to put a stop to it. If not, then we will deal with it when the time comes. Let's not worry, stress, and panic until there is something to worry about. Don made something that smells amazing, would you like to go see what it is? You have to eat."

I reluctantly stood up and made it over to a grave faced Don and two plates. He looked like he wanted to punch the wall out of his own bar, but instead he said, "You need to put on some weight. This here is an 11oz steak and mashed potatoes and gravy. I expect it all to be gone, okay?" I could tell he was serious and his worry about the situation pulled out the *fatherly* side in Don. "Yes sir," I said. He came around the bar and did something that I don't think I've ever seen Don do, he reached out and hugged me. Then backed up and said "I'll shut down the bar for the day and go with you if it comes to that, and I promise you that nobody is getting through me, and I don't think anyone is getting through your buddy here either. You are no longer alone. Remember that, first. Now eat."

We ate, and to be honest, it was the best steak I'd ever had. I finished every bite of everything, and that put a smile on Don's face. Don and Lane kept me talking about anything and everything except what had happened earlier. We stayed late but didn't close it down this time. Lane asked if I was ready to leave, and I guess I was, because I nodded. We waved at Don and headed out the front door. Lane needed clothes so we made the short journey to his apartment, and he packed a bag. I guess that meant he was planning on staying a while, and I was okay with that. We walked through the door, loved on Fritz and played with him for a while, then I sat down, and I wrote about Meagan in the journal. It had been a rough day, so I went ahead and got dressed for bed. Mentally, I was wiped out, so I didn't fight sleep.

I gave Lane a hug and went to bed. He said he was going to stay up and drink another beer or two in the living room to make sure I was okay before he laid down. I could see him sitting there from the bed, watching over me, but it didn't ease the fear building in my gut that something terrible was coming. I had inadvertently put us both in the line of fire from a ghost from my past that I thought was long gone. I didn't know how to deal with that, and my mind gave up and I faded into a deep sleep.

### The Other World

*It was a strange sight. A city like downtown London in the early 1900's that you see in all the scary movies. It was wet, rats were everywhere, there were cobblestone streets, only candlelight, but everyone was dressed in clothing of modern times or so it seemed. The streets were crowded and so loud I could barely*

65

hear myself panting as I was searching for someone that I knew in the sea of faces.

I noticed a girl on the sidewalk at the bottom of a huge staircase that looked like it never ended. The girl was smoking a cigarette and had a blank stare that appeared like it would turn you to stone if she looked at you long enough. I approached the girl and asked if I could bum a smoke. The girl never said anything, never even looked in my direction, but dug into her pocket and produced a cigarette for me.

She handed me a light. As I lit the cigarette, I scanned my surroundings. Everyone was in dark clothing and running around like there was some place they all needed to be, but other than small groups, they were all headed in different directions. Everyone was frenzied and looked panicked, but I couldn't see a reason for panic.

I waved a goodbye to the girl and took off walking at a brisk pace and noticed two men in an alleyway. They were speaking to each other, so I took a chance. "Hello, can you tell me where I am?" I asked. "You are here. We all are here. There isn't a way to be anywhere else. Go see James at the flat off Junction Avenue and he can explain things more clearly, but the biggest thing to remember my dear is that you cannot simply leave here. This place is not a place to visit, but a place to be. So just be," said the boy on the left. He was scrawny with tight black jeans and unruly black hair, but the bluest eyes I had ever seen on another human. "How will I know that I have found James when I get there?" I asked. He made a vague gesture with his hand pointing to the left down a dark street. "When you get there, tell the doorman that Landon sent you. Tell him *you are new here.  He will instruct you on where to go from there," Landon stated.*

*That was odd, I thought.  I was new here, but I didn't know how I had gotten here or where "here" was. Nobody seemed inclined to enlighten me, either.  I tried to remember how it began, but there was nothing to remember.  It was like my mind had been wiped clean. All I could remember was my name.  My name was Delaney.  I said it aloud so it could sink in, and so I could hear how it sounded.  I couldn't even remember purchasing the clothes I was wearing.*

*Trudging off through the wet streets I followed the direction from Landon's hand, and I eventually reached Junction Ave.  Unsure, I looked around and people were still racing to whatever destination they deemed worthy to approach.  I looked up the staircase and saw two men waiting by the door who looked like they were up to no good.  I walked up the towering staircase and noticed a gap at the top of the stairs over a foot wide.  Trying to be brave, I approached them with my head held high.  "Landon sent me to speak to James. I'm new here and would like more information on where I am and why I'm here."  One doorman laughed and showed his yellowed rotting teeth, the other doorman just stared at me with large green eyes, a shirt riddled with holes, and tattered pants.  They were both barefoot.  The one with the bad teeth said "Well, I see you want to join the party" to which I replied "I don't know anything about a party.  I just want to speak to him and learn my purpose here."  Rotted Teeth inquired "Why would you need a purpose?  A purpose is fleeting, you never know where it will lead you or who it will lead you to.  You don't need a purpose.  You need answers that nobody here can give you as we were all dumped here same as you. So, breathe, and join the party. That's what we decided to do, right Bear?"*

*Bear, the one that was decidedly angrier looking than Rotted Teeth, just stared. He almost looked sad. Out of nowhere he grabbed a puppy that was sitting at the top of the stairs taking a bath in the comfort of the shelter hanging over the doorway. Staring straight at me, he dangled the puppy over the gap at the top of the stairs. He smiled at me and dropped the puppy into the hole in the staircase. I screamed but looked down and the puppy had landed and was sprinting away as fast as possible to an unknown location 30 or so feet down at the bottom of the gap. "Why would you do that?! How did the puppy not die?!" I exclaimed. "I did that to demonstrate. It is usually more believable with visual aids. The puppy, like us, cannot die in this place. Believe me many of us have tried repetitively. We have jumped off buildings, stabbed each other, beat each other to what should have caused demise, and nobody dies. When we said you cannot simply leave, that is what we meant. There is no way out of here. No way to get back to where you were before. So, breathe, and join the party like Lou said. Or you could always go sulk and stare into space like some that did not handle the transition as well. Either way, you are stuck here. Suffer or party, it is your choice. You are just a waste of time for James, so leave and find your purpose elsewhere." With that, he spun around and acted like I was no longer standing there.*

*My mouth dropped open in surprise. This can't be happening. This cannot be where I end up. I have no idea how this could have happened. Panic seeped in.*

*My heart started racing. I ran. I rounded a corner and ran right into a man that had to be at least 8 ft tall. He smiled down at me, but it wasn't a welcoming smile. It was the smile of nightmares. His teeth were jagged on the ends and his nose was jutted out and appeared to be sharpened like a knife. When he spoke, he drew out his s's where he almost sounded like a snake. "Where do you think you are going sssssso fassssst? You should really sssssslow down before you bump into ssssssomeone that ain't asssss niccccccce asssssss me." I backed up and pulled my hands up to show I meant no harm. "I'm sorry, I didn't see you there. It won't happen again," I stammered as I backed up to get more space between myself and the threat and then ran around the man. I just wanted some answers. I wanted a purpose. Where was I going to find someone to help me? I stopped, and a rat the size of a well-fed cat ran across my shoe.*

*My mind and heart were racing, and I began to look around and notice faces. I wanted to try to spot someone that looked like me. Someone that looked like they would be nice enough to speak to. Then I remembered the cigarette girl. I spun around and made my way back down the street to try to find her. She was nice enough to give me a cigarette, maybe she could explain things a little better.*

*Cigarette girl was right where I had left her. I approached and said "I think I need your help. Please let me know what is going on and what I can do to get back to my life." Cigarette girl made eye contact with me and stated, "There is no getting home to your life. I had a husband, two kids, 3 dogs, a house with a big yard, a big family, and I'll never see any of them again.*

We were chosen, they say. Chosen to serve in this world for the people who weren't strong enough to endure it. We were cursed with living this never-ending existence until whoever brought us here sees it fit to let us go, and so far, I haven't seen or heard of anyone being let go. We call this person The Collector. They collect us and watch us, but they never release us. Time doesn't exist here, it's always night. My cigarette box never runs out of smokes. My eyes never grow tired. My body never grows weak from standing. We are puppets in a big play that The Collector is putting on and there is no escape. What is your name?" I replied, "Delaney is my name." Cigarette girl responded, "At least you remember your name. A lot of us do not. Some of us come here without remembering anything from our past life. My name is Delia. I remember most of my past. The ones with no recollection have nothing to miss. They party and run around like animals, except animals have more class. Those of us that can remember, the pain is almost too much to bear. The anguish of missing everyone and everything from our previous lives tears us apart every day. We can't stand to look in the mirror for fear we will be reminded of where we came from and the fact that we will never see anyone again. It's as if everyone and everything in your life were to perish, and all you have is yourself and a world full of unknowns. Whoever The Collector is, they don't care about how you feel. We serve a purpose of some kind, but nobody has been able to figure out what that purpose is. Do you want another smoke?"

"Yes, please. This is a lot to take in," I replied with tears staining my dirty cheeks. As I lit the smoke and looked at my surroundings, nothing seemed to have changed. Everyone was still rushing to one destination *or another. Standing there taking deep breaths of smoke, I wondered why I had been chosen. Nobody around me looked familiar, but I couldn't remember anyone to be able to compare either. That meant that everyone around me could be from anywhere or from any period. The Collector had to have been collecting for a long time to have this many people. Now that I knew a little background, looking around, everyone's clothes weren't modern. They appeared to be from all different time periods. They were all wearing just about anything from long dresses to jeans and t-shirts. Now I realized some of these people could have been here for decades. Some for centuries. I could be here for centuries. It was with that realization that I collapsed, and everything went black.*

*When I awoke, Delia was sitting beside me stroking my hair. It took a moment for me to realize again where I was. I remembered snapshots, like still frames, from my past, but nothing of any real substance. I could remember having dogs, and I vaguely remembered the face of a man. Delia hadn't realized that I had awoken and sat there stroking my hair with one hand and smoking a cigarette with the other. I cleared my throat and asked, "What are we going to do, Delia? We can't let The Collector win. We need to figure out who this person or thing is and make it stop."*

*Delia looked frail when she replied, "I have tried. Nobody here has ever seen who The Collector is. They drop us in this other world, and nobody ever receives any answers. Nobody ever gets closure. Since there is nothing physical to fight, nobody ever even gets to try to fight for their freedom from this forsaken place. We simply just exist. Nobody has any real answers." I* looked at her thoughtfully. "What about James?" I asked, feeling hopeful, "When I first spoke to someone, a guy named Landon told me to speak to James, but the guards wouldn't let me in."

"They don't let anyone in to see James," Delia replied with distaste. "Then how do we know that James isn't The Collector?" I asked, holding onto the hope that we were getting somewhere. "No way is James The Collector. I've heard all he does is sit around and drink and eat all day and he has lackeys that make sure he isn't bothered while he parties and does whatever he wants." "I want to see for myself," I said, determined now to find the truth. Delia pulled her hand back and moved over. "Good luck, but I'm not coming with you. James is bad news. That whole building is bad news. If you go back there, you are on your own." I was aggravated that she wouldn't at least offer to help, but I let it slide. "Fine," I replied, "I'll go figure it out myself."

I turned and started back toward Junction Avenue, and I made up my mind that I wasn't leaving without answers. I trudged back up the staircase and walked right up to Bear and Lou. "You will let me in to see James. I need answers and I don't care if he wants to see me or not. We can do this the easy way, or we can do this the hard way." I said this without really having a game plan for what the hard way might entail. Lou smiled with his nasty smile and started to approach me, so I shifted my weight and slid to the side. He got closer than I would have liked, and without thinking I kicked his kneecap and pushed him into the gap at the top of the stairs. He screamed as he made the 30-foot drop and then I heard a definitive thud when he reached the bottom.

Bear rushed at me but stopped short. He either decided that I wasn't worth it, or he was intrigued by what I just did, because the look on his face was a mixture of indecisiveness and what I took as a type of admiration. He backed away from me and opened the big door then stepped aside and bowed and held his arm out as if to show me the way. I stepped past him into total darkness.

There was the flicker of a light way up ahead of me down a very long hallway. I cautiously made my way toward the light. Suddenly a stench hit me so hard, I thought I would pass out from the smell. The hallway was damp, and the smell seemed to be coming from all directions. I continued down the long hallway, and when I got to the end, I realized what was causing the rancid smell.

There was a throne at the end of the hallway with a half-rotted corpse sitting on it. It wasn't until the corpse's head moved to look toward me that I realized this thing was still alive. I threw up all over the floor in front of me. I wasn't sure if it was the smell or the sight of a moving being with rotted flesh peeling off and ooze dripping down this throne onto the floor that made my stomach finally give up the fight.

The thing turned to me and spoke. "I must take from the living in order to stay among the living. I take your dreams, your lives, and I turn you into immortal beings in a land that's sole purpose is to keep me in existence. You want answers, I assume? Well, here are a few. You will not leave this chamber now that you *have entered. You could have lived a mostly normal life, had you kept your curiosity to yourself, but now? Now you are mine. Now you stay with me. And when I'm done with you? You will look like them." At this point, he turned and pointed to the wall in the darkness. "Go, see for yourself what will become of you shortly."*

*It was a short walk to the wall and the smell just got more horrendous. I stifled a scream and choked back another round of vomit when I saw what laid before my eyes. They were mummified bodies. People with their skin still attached, but their bones and muscles all sunken in and their bowels had all been let out right there against the wall. None of them seemed to be alive. I leaned forward, and one of them moved and made a slight moaning sound that reverberated off of the walls in the small room. I looked back toward the throne as he said, "They weren't happy, so I made them suffer for less time. Outside those doors you could live for hundreds of years, but inside here? Inside here you will be dead within the week. Don't worry, I'll make sure you don't suffer any more than they did."*

*He reached out with a staff and knocked me unconscious, while he took his time feeding on me. "This is my world," he thought as he enjoyed his meal. "Nobody can take my world from me."*

# Chapter 6

There were sounds of people bustling around, and beeping. There were lots of beeps, some far and some close by. I couldn't open my eyes, and it felt like something was forcing them to stay shut. I tried to speak and didn't really recognize the sound I was making. I heard Lane's voice close to my ear. He kept saying it was all okay and I needed to relax. Then I started choking and something happened, and I was gasping for breath and finally catching it. My eyes slowly came open and all I could see was white and Lane's face, which looked considerably better than it had last night. Then I looked at his eyes which also looked considerably better, even though the bright lights seemed to still make him squint a little with discomfort. Then it hit me that there were bright lights. Where the hell was I?

"What happened?" I mumbled almost incoherently. Lane looked at me with concern all over his face. "You had a seizure and went into a coma 2 days ago. You had me scared for a while there, and I'm going to need you to quit doing that." He smiled, but the smile looked weak. At second glance, he looked incredibly tired and sad. "I'm so sorry, why are you here? Why didn't you stay at the apartment? Did Fritz stay home alone?" He held his hands up like I was asking too many questions all at one time. "Yeah, like I was going to leave you here all by yourself to let you wake up and not know where you were or what happened. I don't think so, D. You know me better than that. I sent Don with a key to check on Fritz and feed him."

"Well, hello Delaney," said Dr. Baker as she entered the room. "How are you feeling?" I looked up at her and was surprised to see her. "I'm okay, I guess," I replied, though I wasn't sure that I *was* okay. "It was a night terror, wasn't it? I'm guessing a particularly bad one?" I looked down at my hands when she asked that question. "Yeah, it was. I think I died, was dying, or almost died in it." She bought a tiny device over and put it on the table by the bed. "Here is a tape recorder. Lane and I are going to leave you for a bit. I want you to record it so you can write it down later and we can discuss it. Does that sound okay with you?" I picked up the device and looked at it for a moment. Still trying to get my bearings. "Yeah, I guess. It may take a while. It was long." She nodded like she understood and patted my leg under the covers and grabbed Lane by the arm and led him toward the door. "No problem, come on Lane, I'll buy you a coffee." With that, they left me there with the little device.

It took me well over an hour. My head was still fuzzy, but I would remember a detail after I had passed it, so I would just say it whenever I thought of it. I was going to have a heck of a time writing this out once I got home, which hopefully was soon. I felt sorry for Don. He was probably worried sick about me since Lane had told him what happened. I never missed a day at Don's, which I no longer felt sad or depressed about. Don was a great guy, and he did a lot for me just by being there, and now taking care of my boy while I was in here without knowing it. The least I could do was give him regular business. I was sitting there with the recording device on my lap when Dr. Baker and Lane walked back in.

"Did you remember it all?" she asked. "Yeah, I think I got it all. Some of the details came back to me a little late, but I'll fix that when I write it down. When can I go home, Doc?" The look on her face didn't look promising, but she said, "You are free to leave at any time as soon as we do a blood panel on you. I just want to make sure there isn't a vitamin issue or something bigger going on. Your vitals look good though. I want you to stay for observation overnight, but I know you won't agree to that, so I won't beat that particular dead horse today. I would like you to reconsider a sleep study, even if I set up a camera and just have it play on you at your home. I can set the feed to my office, and it will only be my eyes that see what happens. I really think I could help you better if I saw the full picture. Will you at least think about it?"

Lane piped in, "D, do the dang camera. What do you have to lose? You put the camera up, forget it's there, sleep, and then she picks it back up. No harm, no foul. It could potentially help her help you though, which is a big thing. Please." Of course, I couldn't say no to that, so I just nodded my head and told them to set the thing up, but I wanted to go to Don's. She said she would send a tech over, so I told her where I hid my house key. I told her to have him leave it back under the mat when he was finished. She agreed, then we waited on the blood draw, and I got dressed. They always have to wheel you out of the hospital, which I thought was ridiculous, but I was actually pretty weak, so I enjoyed the ride down to the front lobby and out the doors. Then the nurse let me get up and she walked back off into the hospital. Lane looked at me and said, "Hop on," as he turned around and put his arms out. I laughed from the gut, which felt good considering that I hadn't done that in years. "I am not riding piggyback all the way to Don's. No way you are carrying me that far." He raised an eyebrow and looked at me like I was insulting his strength. "You weigh 105 lbs., and you are 5'6". I could carry you like a baby for a mile or more. Just hop on. Don't make me pick you up in front of everyone." I giggled and hopped on his back. I hadn't ridden piggyback with Lane since I was about 10. I think it became *uncool* at some point in time, but I can't remember why. It was actually pretty fun. I was smiling and laughing the entire way.

He put me down outside of Don's and opened the door like he always does to allow me to go first. I found myself thinking that I could get used to someone being around, but in that same thought I find myself mourning when he will eventually leave me. He will eventually want a life, a wife, a home, and most of all to not take care of me. I couldn't blame him for leaving, I just didn't really want him to. I figured I would enjoy it why I could, and cross that bridge when I come to it.

Don came from around the counter and scooped me up and swung me around until I got a little dizzy and threatened to puke on him. At that point he gently sat me down. He was smiling like he just won the lottery, and I was smiling because I just rode piggyback for 4 blocks and then got spun around like I was on an amusement ride. For having zero human contact for the last year, and no loving embraces of any kind the 5 years before that, I was sure getting hugged and touched a lot. To be honest, I enjoyed it. Something about a loving human embrace just made you want to feel better. Don asked if I was free to drink, for which I replied of course, and he slid two beers over to Lane and me.  He said he would be back with a burger and fries for both of us shortly and disappeared behind the wall to the kitchen.

"Your eyes look better, did Dr. Baker give you something?"  He smiled and answered, "She examined me while you were sleeping.  Turns out, one of the antidepressants my doc had put me on a while back causes it in some people.  Not a deadly or a common side effect, so I guess my doctor just didn't know about it and hadn't researched it.  She switched the medication for me and about 24 hours later, my eyes looked somewhat normal again.  I didn't even think of that.  Light still bothers me a little bit, but other than that, I've been doing pretty good for a day or so.  Your doc is a genius."  I smiled back at him and nodded.  "Yeah, she is pretty awesome.  She's helped me through a lot after the surgery and the coma.  She even showed me the best way to part my hair, some hair products to make it grow faster, she goes above and beyond with me every single time.  It's hard to find someone that actually cares these days.  She really took me in at least as much as a doctor can do."  He nodded like he was letting me know he understood.  "I'm glad you found her," he said with a slight smile on his face.

His face looked a lot better than when I had first hurt him.  "Hey," I said, "why don't you stay at your place and just meet me in the morning."  "Are you kicking me out?"  He looked hurt, like I was blaming him for something he didn't know he did.  "No, of course not.  I've just been causing you a lot of trouble since you came back around, and I'd rather that not be what we are all about.  You know?  I want it to go back to good days where we could hang out without a cloud of doom hanging over our heads. I don't want you to ever feel stuck like you have to be around me all the time or I'll break." He shook his head like I had slapped him. "I feel anything but stuck, D. I feel like I finally found somewhere I fit. Like the walls aren't closing in on me anymore. Like I'm not a burden to Mom or anyone else. I missed you more than you could imagine, and I want to be by your side for everything, good or bad. But first, I want you well enough where that can happen, and that's going to take work from both of us, not just you. We are going to need Don too, not just the incredible Dr. Baker. We could possibly even use your parents if you would fill them in on the situation and what's going on. We all love you, and I think you forgot how much we loved you with you being on your own and just surviving for the last 6 years. You have a support system, and you have our hearts. Don't push us away."

Don came around the corner with the burgers and fries and chimed in. "I agree with Lane. You are not a burden or a *cloud of doom* as you say, you are someone that we care about and want to fight right alongside you. Let us fight with you. There is only so much you can do on your own, and if you don't have to do it alone, why would you choose to?" I guess he could hear us talking in the kitchen and wanted to add his opinion.

"Okay, okay. Come home with me. You don't ever have to leave if you don't want to." With that, they both smiled and Don went back into the kitchen for something and Lane picked up his beer. Then Lane did something completely unexpected. He leaned in and kissed me on the lips. Not a kiss that should have been breathtaking by any capacity. It was just a quick peck on the lips, but I could feel my face growing red. I didn't really know what to do or say, so I said, "Okay then, it's settled. You want another round?" He laughed because I was being incredibly awkward as usual and said he would take one.

We stayed at Don's for a while, and then I asked Lane if he would want to walk with Fritz and I to the park. I think I just really wanted to be outside and free before I got videotaped sleeping for the night. I wanted a few more hours of happiness and laughter and Lane before I laid down to whatever might happen next. I couldn't help but wonder if the coma came on because I had died in my dream. I wonder if my physical reaction to that was to seize and almost die in real life. That added one more level of fear to laying down for the night, so I was really just procrastinating. If it were up to me, I'd never sleep again. Sadly, biology wouldn't allow that to work.

We picked Fritz up and walked to the park to sit on the swings and started swinging like we were 10 again. "Did you miss me?" Lane asked. I looked at him while swinging by him and asked, "When?" He rolled his eyes like I had asked a stupid question. "The 6 years we didn't talk. Did you think about me? Or miss me at all?" I turned my gaze to stare out at Fritz running around the park like he owned the place. "Of course, I did. I thought about calling you a lot, but I just never could bring myself to dial. I was afraid of what you would or wouldn't say and whether I would or wouldn't react well. Too many unknowns back then. You were justified in backing off and leaving me alone, but I wasn't justified in letting you, and I knew that. I just figured in hating Justin, you learned to hate me as well.

81

And I don't think I could have survived talking to you when you hated me." He put his arm out and stopped my swing from its climb. "I'm sorry," he started, "I should have made it clear why I wasn't around. We were inseparable most of our lives and cutting that off was the hardest thing I had ever done. Every conversation always turned to you, and people got sick of hearing it. So soon enough, I was all alone and having the same conversation over and over with Mom, which led to me hoping you would call, and then you did. I've been worried sick about you. At least this way, I know for sure if you are okay or not okay, and I'm no longer helpless. D, I love you." We had always told each other we loved each other since we were children, so I wasn't taken by surprise when he said it now. I felt the same way. "Well, I love you too, Lane. You know that." He shook his head and smiled, then got a serious look on his face and looked into my eyes. "No, D. I think I'm in love with you. I think I have been since we were 10. I was angry when you got married because you were getting married in the first place and I didn't have the guts to stop it. Then I was even angrier when he started hurting you. I saw red and I wanted to kill him. Maybe I should have to save you from all of this." I shook my head and looked down at my lap. "Lane, if you would have killed him, you'd be the one in prison and I would be all alone in worse shape, because I would be the reason that you'd never see daylight again. You have always been my rock, and I knew that, whether you were visible or not." Then I shifted back to the bigger issue, but I still couldn't make eye contact with him.

"As far as being in love with me, Lane. You just met me again for the first time in 6 years. You don't know me like you should know me to be in love with me. I love you so much it hurts, but I'm worried that you are in love with me from 6 years ago. What you see now is a broken shell of what I was, but not what I hope to be in the future. What if I change and grow and you decide you only loved the idea of fixing me?" There was a sadness in my voice that even I could hear loud and clear. I wanted so much for him to love me, but I didn't want to end up being hurt again. Ever. "That wouldn't happen, D, and you know that. You have always been my other half, we just never made it official. I always figured that you would turn me down. Is that what you are doing? Are you turning me down?" Exasperated, I shook my head and spoke. "No. I'm postponing this conversation..." and with that he grabbed my face and kissed me for real this time. Like he had been holding it in for the last 16 years of our lives. Like he had been wanting to do it since the day he first laid eyes on me, and I let him. For the first time in years, I let my guard down, loosened up my grip on my solitude, and I let him. Then he leaned back and looked at me like it was the first time he'd ever seen me. I took his hand, and we walked silently back to the apartment. Fritz walked us up the stairs and in the front door as usual and I refilled his food and water, added a treat for extra on top, and gave him some extra love. He hopped on the couch between Lane and I and sat while we turned on the TV to just have a little more time in this day that could have been one of the worst days but was turned into one of the best.

I wasn't ready for it to end, and I sure wasn't ready to be filmed while I was sleeping. I was supposed to call Dr. Baker before I went to bed, so we stayed up until about 10 PM, then I called. She said she was set up and ready.  Game time I guess, but I still wasn't ready.  Lane said he would be right there the entire time and would wake me up the way Dr. Baker told him to if needed.

### *The Battle*

*It was cold.  Severely cold.  I looked down and I was wearing jeans, a t-shirt, and boots, but there was at least a foot of snow all around me as far as I could see.  I was surrounded by dead trees, and everything seemed black and white even though it was in color.  There were no houses, no people, no cars, no roads, nothing as far as the eye could see.*

*There seemed to be some sort of body of water ahead, so I started making my way that direction.  I couldn't really figure out why I wanted to get there, but I did.  I wanted it more than I had ever wanted anything.  I needed to get to the water.  It was like a gravitational pull that was luring me in that I couldn't control.*

*As I made my way closer to the water, I realized there was something there.  Hunched down by the water.  I couldn't tell if it was a person or an animal, but I started walking faster.  I had to see what it was.  I had to get there and felt a sense of urgency.  What if an animal was hurt?  What if someone needed my help?  I had no supplies, but I just knew I had to get there.  If nothing else, to ease my mind.*

*The snow started falling again and it was freezing my eyelashes and my hair.  As I got closer, I* could see it was a man. He was folded up like he was in pain right on the edge of the water. He spoke to me in a pained whisper. "Don't come any closer, please, D. Stay where you are. You can't see this." I knew that voice. Lane. What was Lane doing here? Why was he out here in the freezing cold laying in the snow? "Lane, what is going on? What's wrong?" He turned with an expression of pain I'd never see on his face and said, "Run! D, run! He is here. You have to go, and you have to go fast. You can't turn back, and you can't save me. He is watching and waiting for you to get to me. Go!" My heart began to race, but I stayed where I was. "Lane, who is he? Get up and go with me. We can both go. There has to be some place close by to lay low."

"There is nowhere to hide. You have to keep running and run fast. I'd slow you down, he caught me first. Please, go. Please, D, go!" He was pleading, but I wasn't listening, and I sure wasn't leaving him there. Not this time. I wasn't running anymore. "Who is he, Lane? Is it Justin? Is he out?" Lane looked resigned when he met my eyes. "He got out yesterday, and I am begging you to run. He wants blood. He is using me to get you here." I shook my head. "That makes no sense, Lane. I didn't even know you were you. It wouldn't have done him any good if I had gone the other way. Get up, let's go." "I can't." He stated defeatedly. He turned over and put his legs out. The Achilles tendon on both of his legs had been slashed. He wasn't going anywhere unless I carried him. Instead of fear, a rage I had never known before rose inside of me. "Where the hell is he, Lane? Which way did he go?" I scanned as far as I could see in every direction. "He went into the water. I don't know how, but I still feel him there."

*The water. Water has always been my safe and calm place, and so had Lane. He wasn't going to take either of them from me. Not now. Not today. Not like this. I no longer felt cold. I was burning up inside and out. I walked towards the water. I felt like it should have been frozen, but steam was coming from the top of it like it was a hot spring. "Drag yourself back Lane. Get to the tree line. I'll take care of it." He panicked. "D, please stop. You can't win against him, he'll kill you. I can't lose you, please come back to me." I was adamant this time. This wasn't going to happen again. It would never happen again. "No. Drag yourself to the tree line. And, hey Lane?" He looked up at me, eyes still pleading. "Yeah?" He said through gritted teeth. "I love you too." With that I walked into the water.*

*I marched in like I owned the lake and all the land around it. I went under the surface, and almost immediately saw Justin's face. He stared straight into my eyes out of the greenish hue of the water. I could breathe, and so could he. All the water really did was make everything move in slow motion. There were fish around us, and most of them were huge and some had teeth as big as my fingers, but I didn't fear them, and I didn't fear him. An entire foot of water around my body was bubbling like it was just as angry as I was. The water was boiling around me as if to warn him of my anger and what I was actually capable of.*

*I leaned in and grabbed him by the collar. He smiled. At that point, I looked over into the depth of the water and I saw the head of a fish the size of a Volkswagen with teeth like butcher knives. I smiled and nodded my head slightly as if asking the fish to come to me. The beast started swimming slowly my direction* and got up close to me and bowed its head. I ordered the beast to attack, and it followed my orders. I was the alpha down here somehow. Everything was warm, and every creature bent to my will. The beast wasn't the only one that heard my order. From everywhere in the deepest depths around us, creatures came to light and attacked and shredded Justin piece by piece. He wasn't smiling anymore, in fact there wasn't much of a face to show a smile even if he wanted to.

I walked back out of the water slowly. Reaching out the entire way to pet the creatures that had assisted me in battle if that's what you could even call it. It was more of an assassination, but I'll take it either way. Justin was no longer a threat, and I was heading out to get Lane to safety.

As I made it to the shore, heat was still pouring off me even though I was drenched. Lane looked at me like I was a ghost. I helped him up, and we set off for the path behind the small lake. There was a barn in the distance with a small house in front. I walked Lane all the way to the porch, and then I sat him down, and went up to knock. Joe answered the door. "Why are you here, Joe?" I was still angry, and I was still out for blood if it came down to it. "Did you kill him? Did you finish it?" he asked with no emotion on his face at all. "Yeah, Joe. He's gone. He hurt Lane pretty badly, can we come in and get him warmed up and call an ambulance please?"

"Justin didn't do that to Lane. I did. Justin needed bait. I provided the bait. Let's see just how strong you are on land." Joe grabbed me by the shirt and pulled me into the shack and slammed me into the fireplace. He grabbed a fire poker that had been in the fire and raised it in front of my face. He said, "Good luck. Truly. I hope you come out on top, but you have to know why I have to go down fighting. It's about blood."

I hadn't been expecting this. At all. The poker got closer and closer to my cheek, and then he pressed it to my flesh. The searing skin smelled scorched almost immediately. The smell of it burning made me want to throw up, but I fought the urge to move and inched my hands down the fireplace and found the handle of the shovel in the fireplace tool kit. I grabbed it with my left hand and brought it up with all my strength underneath his chin. It didn't do much damage, but it backed him up a few feet, even though it didn't make him drop the poker.

"There she is. The fighter. Too bad you waited this long to defend yourself. You could have really been someone instead of what you have become, Delaney. Now the world will never know." He charged at me with the poker held out in front of him like a spear. I waited until the last minute and dodged the blow, grabbed the back of his neck and pushed his face into the fire, then pushed on his back as hard as I could to keep it there. His screams were ear piercing and didn't even sound human.

I picked up the fire poker, and I started swinging it with everything I had, hitting him over and over until he didn't move anymore. Not only did he not move, but his head was still in the fire. He was gone. The fight was over. I went out and helped Lane get into the house. The smell was making both of us sick and was extra strong for me considering the entire left side of my face had at least 3rd degree burns from the fire poker. I had been branded, but I didn't care. I had won. I *grabbed the phone and called for an ambulance and a mortician. The person on the other line told me it would be an hour or two, but they would get someone out as soon as possible.*

*I got Lane up on a bed and looked at the backs of his feet. I was scared to cauterize the wound just in case it could be repaired. So I wrapped it in gauze and got some ice from the freezer and put it in bags and gently slid the bags under both of heels.*

*Lane looked at me, and cupped my face, and said "D, let me look at your burns. Turn to the side." He rubbed some ointment on the side of my face and added some gauze but didn't tape it. The ointment was keeping it on, and I think we were both worried my face would peel off with the tape. "Thank you for saving me. Come lay with me." I curled up in his arms on my right side to save my face from getting in worse shape by touching the sheets and drifted off in his embrace.*

I woke to Lane smiling from ear to ear at the foot of the bed. I asked, "What?" He got a goofy grin on his face and said, "You were saying my name. A lot. It was kind of nice to hear, unless you were kicking my ass. If that is the case, then who won?" I laughed and rolled over and covered my head with a blanket. It was only in my dreams, but I got to fall asleep without worrying in his arms, and it had felt nice. It all had felt nice. I woke with a sense of strength and hope, and even with Lane teasing me, I felt like it was going to be the start of a good day.

I couldn't have been more wrong.

# Chapter 7

I got out of bed, with Lane watching me the entire time, and walked into the kitchen to get my notebook. I wrote down the night terror. I had no bruises and no real damage at all. I wondered to myself if it was because I had won the battle this time. If I had lost in the night terror, is that when I would have started thrashing and hurting myself? I wasn't sure of the answer to that, but it seemed to be a solid guess that winning or losing had something to do with the outcome of my physical state. If I stay on the winning side, maybe I can pull myself out of the terrors after all. I at least had a little hope for the first time in a very long time. Lane kept bugging me and asking why I kept saying his name.

"You were there, Lane. That's all." I was smiling at him but was slow to share with him. I was afraid he would interpret it the wrong way. "Was I a hero in this one? Did I save the day?" I decided to mess with him a little. "Actually, I saved *you*. How does that make you feel?" He smiled a different smile and said, "Well, honestly, it sounds pretty hot. You saved me, huh? How did that happen?" So, I decided to go ahead and explain the dream to him. His smile faded quickly. He asked, "How many nights has he been in your night terrors?" I thought for a minute, and then replied, "Actually, that was the first time, I think." He didn't look happy with that answer. "This doesn't make you wonder if he is going to pop up out of the blue today? I mean you had a night terror about me, and we spoke the day after." I shook my head. "Yeah, we spoke because I called you. It's not fate, Lane. I'm not a fortune teller, psychic, or a mind reader. I'm just human like anyone else. I have no idea what it means, but I can almost guarantee you Justin will not be anywhere near me today. He is locked up. And I think Joe got the hint when Don gave him the boot. I don't think it's going to be an issue, so can we please just enjoy the day?"

I was pushing the thought away, but that nagging feeling was still there in the back of my mind. Lane surrendered. "Yeah, sorry, you are right. Let's enjoy the day." He got up and walked to the window and turned back and said, "Why don't we do something different today?" I was skeptical. "Different because you want to do something different with me? Or different because you don't want to be at Don's in case someone comes by looking for me?" He shrugged and asked, "Can it be both?" "Yeah, I guess it can," I said, even though I was getting aggravated.

There was no way my dreams had anything to do with the future. Lane's eye situation just happened to be a coincidence and turned out it wasn't a major thing any way. Dr. Baker had him fixed up and probably didn't even charge him for it within 24 hours of trying. He wasn't dying, there was no plague, there was nothing similar about it at all except he couldn't go outside in daylight. There's no way I could have predicted that in any way.  Plus, I think about Lane a lot, so it had to just be a coincidence.  That's all.  Nothing more to it.

I turned to Lane and said, "How about we do the regular today, just to prove you are wrong about this psychic thing, then we can do something different tomorrow.  Deal?"  It was his turn to look annoyed now.  "It's bugging you now, isn't it?  You think there might be something to it."  I shook my head and stuck by my denial.  "No, Lane, I don't think there is anything to it.  I just want *you* to see that there is nothing to it.  So can we drop it and go grab some food at Don's and hang out with him like *normal*?"  He looked defeated and exhausted.  "Sure, D.  Whatever you want to do.  Let's go."

We had both gone from playful and happy to on edge and cranky in just a few hours.  He couldn't be right.  This couldn't be a thing.  I hadn't met anyone from any of the other terrors, though Meagan did kind of resemble Delia from a couple nights ago, they weren't the same person, nor the same circumstances, and I saw Meagan before I dreamt of Delia.  It was all going to be okay, and Justin and Joe were not going to make appearances.  All would be fine.

Except it wasn't.

Lane opened the door to Don's for me with a little less enthusiasm than he had used before, but I walked through just the same, and found 3 officers sitting at the bar.  There were never cops in here, it wasn't really a cop-type bar, but here they sat.  They all looked up at me and stared with eyes that had something to say but were drawing straws to see who actually wanted to be the one to talk.

"Are you Delaney?" The one on the back stool said as he stood up to face me. "Yes sir, that's me. Delaney Jameson. Is everything okay? Where's Don?" I was getting more and more concerned. "Who is that with you?" Lane stepped forward slightly and said, "Lane Davidson, sir." "Okay," the same officer replied. "Why don't you two come on in here and have a seat in a booth so we can talk for a minute. You are *together,* right?" Lane looked at me for an answer, and I said, "Yes sir, Lane is with me." The officer nodded slightly in approval. "Okay then, come over here and have a seat."

The group stood and, as a whole, walked us over to the 8-seater booth. I guess so we would all have a little room, considering there was only 5 of us. I don't know that I'd ever seen this booth fully occupied before. I sat there with a pit in my stomach and searching in the background for Don, but not finding him.

The main officer laid a packet on the table in front of me. "Delaney, this here is a will and testament from Don Stills. He says in here that if anything should happen to him, you are his sole heir and beneficiary. Does that sound right to you?" My heart skipped a beat. Don had always told me I was the daughter he never had, but I didn't think he meant it like that. I mean, why choose me for that kind of thing? Why would it matter anyways? Why weren't they telling me where Don was? My head was spinning, and my hands were shaking and sweaty. "Well, sir, we were really close. I spent almost every day with him. Can you please tell me what happened?  Is Don okay?"  He looked almost bashful when he stated, "Ma'am I have several troubling things to go through with you, and I promise I will get to those, but I need to make sure you are who you say you are first.  Can you show me your ID please?"  I pulled out my wallet and handed my ID over.  Before he could ask him for it, Lane did the same.  He looked them over and then handed them back with a slight nod, like his curiosity was satisfied.

"At around 4:30 AM, one Justin Walker was being transported to the hospital due to being stabbed repeatedly in what appeared to be a gang brawl in lockup.  During transport, a truck blocked the road in front of the ambulance and the guards that were riding with the prisoner didn't have a clear view from the back of the vehicle.  We only had the one vehicle, due to the prisoner not being considered a flight risk of any significance due to his physical state.  One of the guards exited the transport vehicle and walked around to see what the issue was, and the guy at the wheel pulled a knife and killed him, to spare you the details, miss.  Long story short, Mr. Walker got away.  The driver of the vehicle that blocked the road according the report taken at the scene, is believed to be his brother Joe Walker.  We believe the entire thing was a setup, miss.  Including the gang fight."

My heart sank and I jumped up and ran to the trash can and threw up.  This can't be happening.  It just can't be happening.  This kind of crap happens in bad movies or cop shows, but not in life.  Not for real.  Lane stood behind me with one hand holding my hair back and the other stroking my back.  I finished and then we went back and took our seats and one of the other officers brought me and Lane both a glass of water. They waited for me to gain a little composure, and then they continued.

"I'm afraid there is more. It appears they both came straight here. There is a tape. Don had security cameras put in after that break-in about 2 years ago and we are thankful that they were still connected to record for 24 hours at a time before it deletes it. I contacted the company this morning and got multiple copies of the tape. It appears Don had stayed late after closing to do some deep cleaning, or he would have been home and most likely safe. I'm going to save you the details again, ma'am, but Don passed away about 3 hours after the beating he received from the Walkers. I'm terribly sorry. The bar, his truck, and his house out on Sheridan all belong to you now. A lawyer will be by shortly with the paperwork for the property, which is why we are all here. To meet the lawyer, to intercept you, and to make sure that the Walkers don't come back."

Tears started coming and they didn't stop. I couldn't breathe. I felt like someone was sitting on my chest. Don had died because of me. He was gone, and that was my fault. He left me the bar and his house. I didn't even know he had a house. I had no idea where or how he lived. I knew the bar did okay and it was paid off. I knew he was retired and didn't really need the money, but the conversation never really got much farther. Sometimes I think he just kept the bar open so I'd have somewhere to go and someone to talk to. I had to know more. I had to know what they had done to him. The anger inside me started to well up and take over.

"Did he fight?" I asked with an expressionless tone. "Ma'am?" the officer replied looking confused. "Did Don fight them? Did he get some punches in? Did he fight for his life?" I needed to know that he had fought back. I needed to know they didn't just take him out. I wanted to be sure he got his two cents in before he was gone. "Yes ma'am. He fought. He did some damage too. It all took place in the back room behind the kitchen, and we can't let you go back there yet, but the answer is yes. He fought like hell. If there would have been just one on one, he probably would have won." I nodded once. Just a final motion. Something to keep myself grounded to the thought that Don could have killed Justin if he had gone alone. I looked into the lead officer's eyes. "I want to see the tape," I said. The officer immediately started shaking his head and put his hands up in a gesture trying to get me to reconsider what I was asking for. "Ma'am I don't believe that's a good idea. It's pretty brutal." He was fighting himself on the idea. He knew I could potentially assist, but he didn't want to put me through it. "I know what the Walker boys look like. I need to see that it's Justin and Joe. At least show me that part." He fished out a tablet and brought it to life and froze the screen where I could see it. It was grainy and not the best picture but standing right there looking at the camera was Justin and Joe. Justin bandaged up from his fight that was most likely staged. No mistaking either of their faces, though. I'd never forget them as long as I lived. "It's them," I said. I felt so defeated. This can't be happening. I had gone into crisis mode, and Lane was just letting me do what I needed to do to keep from falling apart.

"Sir, do you know who I am? Do you know what Justin Walker did to me?" I asked the main officer that I'd been speaking to. "Yes, ma'am. I do." He looked down at his hands, but I kept my eyes up, glaring into the top of his eyelids. "Then what is your advice. As an officer of the law that couldn't stop the man, keep him locked up, or keep him from killing one of two friends I have. How do I stay alive?" The officer looked up and looked resigned, but thoughtful. "I would advise you to stay armed if you are familiar with guns. Keep yourself safe at all costs, and as soon as it turns to self-defense, defend yourself with everything you have. If Don was one of two friends you have, I would venture that you two are the next on the Walkers clean up list. Do you have guns or at least something to defend yourself with?" I nodded with finality and replied. "Yes," I said, a little too quickly for Lane. Lane spoke for the first time, "D, do you really think that's a good plan? To get a gun and wait until you know for sure you are defending yourself, because by law it has to be self-defense to keep you from going to prison. Then, on top of everything else, you'd be shooting him and hoping that he actually dies and doesn't go back to prison where he could possibly get out and start this whole thing over again?"

"Well that's true, but seeing as how I am saying that you both are in mortal danger, and he is an escaped fugitive from the justice system, I would say you could plead self-defense pretty easily," the officer stated. Lane wasn't sold on the idea. "Or with a good defense attorney they could turn it into a revenge killing by a disgruntled ex-girlfriend who was almost killed by the guy, and also best friends with someone the guy allegedly killed. There is always a spin on things.

Always an angle. Tread carefully, D. I don't want to see you hurt, and I *would* go to prison for you, but I'd rather not."

"Do I have another option?" I asked the officer. He thought for a moment and then shrugged his shoulders. "I'm not sure what it would be. Hand-to-hand fighting, if you can get with someone to assist you with some self-defense techniques, but all in all, I would feel better knowing you were armed just in case." Lane relaxed a little. "I know some things about self-defense, and I also know a family thought would defend you with every last breath they had, D." He let that idea hang in the air. "Roger, keep an eye on these folks while I go make some calls, please. And watch the door for the lawyer. He should be here any minute now. I'll be right back." He spun around and walked out of the door. The officer called Roger took the seat of the absent officer. I looked at Lane, and he wrapped me in a hug, and I sobbed some more.

The Lawyer arrived. He was a tall elderly man named Jerry Simmons. He was polite and quick. He brought in the paperwork and went through it quickly, handed me keys to the bar, a house, and a Ford Bronco, the old beefy kind, and told me he wished me the best of luck and if I had any questions to call him on the number that was listed on the card that he handed me. I was the next of kin, so on top of learning how to defend myself against a worst-case scenario, I was assuming I'd also have to plan a funeral. I'd never done that before, but I figured it was something that fell on the next of kin. I asked Jerry before he walked out the door, and he said Don hadn't wanted me to worry with it and all the arrangements had been made beforehand.

I would be notified when it was settled, and I would be the only one notified once they were complete, for obvious reasons. With that, he walked out the door.

Don deserved more than just Lane and I at his funeral, but I didn't have the energy to deal with it right then. Don would just say he was dead, what did it matter to him? In fact, he had said that many times before. I needed to focus. Justin and Joe were out there, and they were coming after Lane and I if they were stupid. If they were smart, they'd be halfway to Montana by now and never look back, but nobody ever accused the Walkers of being smart. They were honestly probably watching the place right now. Waiting for a chance to get me alone, which wasn't going to happen, for multiple reasons. One main reason was, I was going to bite the bullet and call home like Lane had subtly advised earlier. I needed reinforcement and I had parents and a few brothers of my own that, even if they truly hated me, would run to assist in a situation like this. They wouldn't be able to say no. Blood. It's a weird bond.

I hadn't seen or heard from my brothers since I married Justin. They knew him, didn't approve, and decided they didn't want to pretend to. Which, oddly enough, would really work to my advantage right now. I figured I'd have the best luck with Jace. I was always his favorite, even if he never outwardly admitted to it. I picked up my cell phone and stared at it for a minute. Then I told Lane it was time. He knew exactly what I meant. I dialed my estranged brother's number from memory.

I put it on speaker so Lane could hear the exchange and pop into the conversation, if needed. I wasn't sure how this was going to go. Jace answered on the second ring with a clipped tone. "Yeah?" I rolled my eyes a little. My loving brother, always the polite one. "Hey Jace. It's D." There was silence, then a sigh. "What's wrong?" he asked. I tried not to take offense that after all these years, he knew I'd only call if I was in some sort of trouble. "It's a long story, but here are the highlights. Justin almost killed me a year ago. I got a divorce from him, and he went to jail, but broke out and killed one of the two friends that I have this morning. Police are telling me to get a gun and learn how to fight. He's out for blood. Joe is with him." There was a brief moment of silence, and then he asked, "Where are you?" I straightened a little and answered, "Don's in downtown Tulsa. I can send you the directions." No hesitation from him. "I'll be there in 45. I'm bringing at least Luke, but probably Dad too." It was a statement. Not a question. He needed backup as well, and our family was known back home for handling our own. "Thank you, Jace." "Yup," he said and then there was a final beep letting me know that my brother had ended the call.

"I take it he is the quiet type?" Roger asked. Lane replied, "Jace never really had much to say unless there was something to say. He doesn't waste words. He's more of an action kind of guy. Right, D?" I nodded, remembering plenty of times my brother had jumped into action at my defense. "Yeah. He always was," I said. I looked down at my lap. "Lane, I think he was mad." Lane shook his head. "Nah, D. He doesn't get mad. He is like you. He goes into crisis mode and fixes the problem, which in this case is a big problem. His wheels were turning, is all. Don't get yourself worked up until there is something to get worked up about." I sighed and slouched back into the booth. "I know you are right, but it still worries me. It's been over 6 years since I've seen them. Hugged them. Told them I love them. Then the first time they hear from me, it's because I'm so far in over my head that there's a real chance that I may not survive this. They have to come, but they probably don't want to come." Roger stepped in, "From experience, I have a daughter myself who has a hard head, your family loves you. Even if they don't show it the way they used to show it. They are most likely breathing a sigh of relief that you are away from that guy, and they got to hear your voice. If they are hurt, it's because of what happened a year ago, and this is the first they are hearing of it. Time heals that pain, though. Time and love heal these things better than most things do."

It was at that point that I decided I liked Roger. I went to the bar and grabbed two beers for Lane and I. I sat back down, cradled my beer, thought about Don, and waited for whatever was coming from the small town I was raised in. I had a feeling they were going to bring hell with them, and for once, I was okay with that.

# Chapter 8

Well, Jace didn't just bring Dad and Luke, he brought about everyone in our inner circle of family.

My Uncle, my 3 brothers, Dad, and my cousin were all in tow. It was like a family reunion, but not the good kind. They stepped into Don's like they owned the place. Dad was a big man, about 6'5" and toned muscle. He worked hard every day of his life and hadn't even begun to stop that routine. Jace and Luke were built like Dad, just on a slightly different scale. Jace was the tallest at 6'6", and he didn't have the muscles that 30 extra years had earned Dad, but he wasn't scrawny either. Luke was 6'3" and serious as a heart attack. Always had been. James, or Jamie as I called him, was different. He was about 6 foot flat with boots on, and he looked and acted like Momma. My cousin Greg had grown up as a brother to me as well. He had a calm soul, but I'd seen him get into his share of bar fights growing up and word got around pretty quickly that you didn't want to be on the receiving end of any punch he could throw. His dad, Uncle Rex, was a tough man and built like an ox. I was the only girl in my immediate family other than the mommas. I was starting to wonder how they hadn't all found me and dragged me back before now. It looked like the rodeo was in town with all of them in one room. From behind them, I saw a small figure making her way to the front. Momma. She had come with them, which I guess I should have known. She hadn't seen me in 6 years, and she raised us to know that family always came first, no matter the circumstances. She wasn't about to let anyone hurt any of her kids unless it was her.

"D. You look too skinny. Is there a place we can eat close by? We have a lot to talk about." A room full of big muscular men, and Momma still had the most dominant presence in the room. "Yeah, Momma, let's go down the street. There's a burger shack with tables big enough we may get to sit together. We can't access the kitchen here yet, and none of ya'll ever really liked my cooking anyhow." They parted to let me through, and Mom grabbed me on the way by and pulled me in for the biggest hug. I'd forgotten again that people hug on a normal basis. I hadn't gotten used to it yet, which probably came off as rude, but was just new to me in this part of my life. I had grown so use to not being touched affectionately and then not being touched at all for the last year, that I was having to relearn the basic human interactions that when I was growing up were second nature. I hugged her back, and she smiled a weak smile then let me lead the way after she took a second to hug Lane and ask him about his face. I thought to myself it was a good thing she didn't see it a few days ago, but either way, I had a lot of explaining to do.

To their credit, they didn't all attack with questions at once. They listened to the last 6 years of my life in a nutshell asking questions along the way as warranted. Jace was getting angrier and angrier. His face was bright red like he was about to have a stroke. I put my hand on his and assured him I was okay several times throughout the timeline. When I got to the incident, Momma flinched, and I saw tears in her eyes. Of course, the first question after that was why hadn't I called them? I didn't have a good answer. I didn't have an answer at all, so I just told them I wasn't sure they wanted to hear from me, and I didn't want to worry them. There was silence for several minutes, and then Jace looked up and said, "I'll kill him."

"You will do no such thing. At least, not unless you have to. You hear me, son?" Momma said. He looked at her and replied, "Ma, there is nothing he can say or do short of turning himself in to the police that will keep him alive now." Nobody said anything. I looked up and said, "We have another issue. I live in a one-bedroom loft, and there are 7 of you." Dad looked up and patted the air like he was telling someone to sit down. "Don't worry about that, D. We brought 3 RVs and are staying in the RV park down the street from here, but at least 2 of us will be with you at all times," Dad said. Hearing him speak for the first time in 6 years brought tears to my eyes. I was always a Daddy's girl. I think it's basically a rule that you have to be a Daddy's girl if you are the only girl and have 3 brothers, but I always loved him for not treating me any different than the guys. I worked just as hard on the farm growing up and kept up with the boys. Even as small as I was, Dad never acted like a job was too big for me to do. He pushed me and molded me into a confident young woman, and now look at me. I was falling apart, weak, broken, and no confidence. Funny how one person can change into another person over half a decade. I was going to have to make a point to get stronger. To be the woman I was raised to be, but it wasn't going to happen today. So, I just sighed and turned to Luke.

"Thank you for coming. I know you and Joe used to be close, and I know this is hard on you to see them this way. I verified from the video that it was Justin and Joe myself, or I wouldn't have accused them. You know that, right?" He looked up and with a resigned look on his face said, "Joe changed, D. He changed whenever we all turned on Justin. Blood. It's a bond that isn't easily broken. The first time Justin hurt you should have been the last time, but for reasons unknown you stayed, and you almost paid the ultimate price for that mistake. Now, we just have to get back to where we were. All of us. We were all hurt and broken these last 6 years, D. Not just you. It took a toll on the entire family every holiday, birthday, really any time we got together. The stories always turned to you, then everything would change, and nobody would want to celebrate. We felt like we all let you down by letting you walk down the aisle in the first place. We all knew he was bad news, but none of us kidnapped you, so that's on us too. You were always so dang hard-headed, that even though we were worried about you, we all just kind of figured you'd handle it if it got too bad. It never dawned on any of us until today, that you weren't quite as strong as we had built you up to be in our heads. You were the best of all of us in one small little package. Don't you ever leave us like that again. And Lane? If you ever let her, I'll come after you with everything I've got. And I've got a lot. Do you understand? Both of you?" I backed my chair up and walked around the table and put my arms around my brother's neck and pecked him on the cheek. "I won't ever disappear again by choice, Luke. I can promise you that. I missed you all and I love you all so much. We were the toughest family in town back in the day, and I think we can still be, even though it's a bigger town up here." He smiled and I went around and sat back next to Lane.

Jace looked at me with concern on his face and said, "Lane said you hit him. In your sleep. Like some kind of fit while you were out. What's going on with that? Does it happen every night? Is it because of the injury or because of all the stuff that happened before?" Several loaded questions coming in at one time. I forced my head up and said, "Night terrors. I have them basically every time I fall asleep. Lane's been trying to help me figure them out, same as my doctor. They started after the head injury, but the doc thinks it could be the trauma mixed in with the injury that set them off. I can't shut it off. It's safest not to sleep in the same room with me." I lifted my sleeves and showed them the scars and bruises, and Momma looked like she was holding her breath. "They don't really hurt, Momma. I'm fine. I don't know what I'm doing when I do it. Dr. Baker videoed me last night while I was sleeping but so much has happened, I haven't been able to call her yet. I should probably go do that now. I'll be back."

I walked away and went outside the restaurant and dialed Dr. Baker. She asked if I had written down what happened, and I said I had. She asked what was different this time, and I had told her I won. I don't normally win anything in my night terrors especially not like some kind of warrior, but I had faced this one head-on and come out on top. There was no second guessing who was the threat and no hesitation that I would eliminate that threat. I told her that I thought that was the difference and why it wasn't so bad. She said she wanted to leave the cameras up for a few more nights to review and asked if that was okay, and I told her it was. I filled her in on what had happened this morning and what was going on, and she was concerned that the extra stress would make them worse and that was dangerous considering my recent predicament. I told her my entire family is in town, and that I was safe. She seemed to like the idea that I had the common sense to call them. I assured her I would be fine and then hung up with her and returned to the table.

"So, you own a bar, house, and a Bronco?" Jamie asked when I sat back down. I nodded but looked down as tears formed in my eyes thinking of Don. "Yeah. My friend they killed left his estate to me. All of it. Not sure what I will do with it, but I know he had more regulars than just me, so I may keep the bar open and run it myself. I was there all the time anyway and served whenever he was in the back cooking, so it won't be much of a stretch." Dad chimed in with the authority he was known for, "You aren't running anything until the Police are done with it and Justin is behind bars. At least, not without us being there with you. I don't trust anyone. Justin has a lot of friends in low places and apparently made more on the inside. This whole situation was planned, and he had help. You all understand that? Nobody goes unarmed, and nobody leaves D entirely alone. At all. Not even while she is sleeping, so Jace you might want to go buy us some helmets, so we don't all end up looking like Lane over there." Dad grinned. It was his attempt at a joke and to lighten the mood, and it worked. We all smiled and loosened up a little bit. He added, "Good to know you still remember how to fight, even if you are unconscious when you do so. Jace, Luke, and Jamie will work with you on some self-defense techniques, and you are going to do as that officer said and carry a gun with you everywhere. You know how to handle a gun and in the great state of Oklahoma, we have Constitutional carry. Carry it everywhere, D. I mean it. Rex, can you touch you up on your gun handling and grab one of mine out of the truck and give it to you. I'm going to make a couple of calls. I have an old friend that works up there at the prison, and I want to see what he can tell me about this fight. It's going to be alright, D. It's all going to be alright."

I had a strange sense of strength come over me. A little spark brought a piece of the old me forward. I wasn't fragile. I wasn't scared. I was a Jameson. Our entire family has always been taught to run towards the fight, not away with the rest of the crowd. We handle problems, we don't avoid them. It's about damn time I remember how strong I am, pick myself up out of this 6-year grave, dust myself off, and get busy. I stood up, walked around the table, and ran into my dad's arms. He held me tight for a few moments, then put his hands on my shoulders and held me at arm's length. "Sis, you can do this. You've always had it in you to protect yourself. You leave the beaten down version of you in the very back of your mind and bring the fighter out. This is your fight, and this is your chance to stand and look evil in the face and show it what you are made of. You show the Walkers that you aren't a little girl, you are my daughter, and you are stronger than all my boys put together. I'll be back in a few minutes, okay? Come on, Rex."

Dad and Uncle Rex walked out the door. I told Momma I needed to go to the apartment to take a shower and change into more suitable clothes. I needed something more comfortable and agile than what I was wearing if I was going to be moving a lot. She said she would go with Lane and I and then looked at Jace and Greg and told them both to come as well. Luke and Jamie stayed behind with Uncle Rex and Dad to plan strategy.

As we walked outside, Uncle Rex came over with a Taurus 9mm and I checked it, then tucked it away in my waistband.   Behind me, Jace was giving Lane a hard time about getting beat up by the tiniest girl he'd ever fought, and they were all laughing.  Momma and I took off walking with the boys trailing behind us keeping an eye out.  For a few minutes it was nice, almost peaceful.  At that moment, I knew Don would be proud of me for calling them and leaning on someone. We were finally a family again, and it felt so great to be a part of a family for the first time in 6 years with Lane by my side.

We made it to the apartment, and I got in the shower.  I just stood there for the longest time letting the hot water wash away the last 6 years and clear my mind for what lay ahead.  I didn't have to stay and fight. Lane and I could go back home with the family.  I could find somewhere to live in a little house out in the country.  But, with that being said, I couldn't bear to leave Don's, not just yet.  That man had built and ran the bar for longer than I had been alive.  His blood, sweat, and tears went into that place, and he had left it to me.  I made a mental note to go check out his house at some point that evening.  I got out of the shower and toweled off.  Put some product in my hair and walked out to my bedroom in my towel.  I made sure the door was locked and got dressed.  I had to think range of motion, so I got a pair of my old work jeans that had plenty of room in them considering the weight I'd lost, and they were worn in, so they were comfortable.  I grabbed a hoodie off the rack to put on over my t-shirt to cover the gun better and grabbed a pair of Converse from the closet.  Now, I could fight if I needed to.  I was comfortable, clean, and ready to go except for one thing.  My hair.  It was down to my butt and unruly, which is how I usually liked it, but not for today.  I walked into the living room and turned to Momma. "Could you French braid my hair? I'd rather it be out of my way with everything going on." She smiled like I had just asked her if she wanted to go to a party with me. "No problem, come sit in the floor and I'll sit behind you. Let's do twin braids so I can get them in tighter, okay?" I nodded and smiled back. "Thanks Momma," I said as I tucked in on the floor and sat cross-legged at my mom's feet.

It took her close to an hour to get the mess that was my hair under control. When it was done, it looked perfect. Like I was ready to work. Jace smiled, "Ladies and gentlemen, looks like D is back in business." I snickered and walked to the bedroom to get my gun and tucked it in my waistband again and pulled the hoodie down over it. I was ready.

We made our way downstairs and back to Don's and found Officer Roger and the officer that told me to stay armed waiting for us there. "Miss, we are finished with the crime scene, and your dad and your uncle are in back cleaning it up. Your dad informed us that you knew your way around firearms, but for your safety and my peace of mind, I'd like to walk through some things with you to be sure. My name is Officer John Harold. I got permission from the captain to take you and Lane to the range at headquarters and make sure you know how to shoot correctly and are comfortable. Is that plan okay with you?" I nodded my head, anxious to get some practice in. It had been years since I held a firearm. "Yes sir, that sounds great. Thank you for all your help. You too, Officer Roger." With that, he escorted Lane and I to a police car, and opened the door for us. Out of respect, I told him I was carrying, but he already knew. Uncle Rex had even told him the make of the gun already. Lane slid in beside me, and then Momma walked up and said she was going too. So, we all squeezed in the back and John took off down the road.

The drive to headquarters didn't even take 5 minutes. We probably could have walked it just as fast even with all the stoplights involved, but we arrived in one piece and Officer John opened the doors so we could get out and go inside. The range was indoors in the basement of the police precinct. He stopped at the counter and picked up 4 boxes of ammunition for the guns they had set out for us, and then he led us down the long sterile hallway to the stairs and down into the range. We had it all to ourselves, which I'm sure was part of the planning on Officer John's part. He wanted no interruptions. He walked me through basic safety, got me glasses and head gear, watched me load the gun and check it, then he asked me to aim at the target.

The target was a slip of paper on a peg that was outlined like a man with circles on it on the opposite side of the room. I picked the gun up, aimed, and asked where he would like me to hit the target. He said, "Take a gut shot. Aim right for center mass. You are free to fire." I aimed, breathed in, and then let it out really slowly relaxing my muscles and my mind, then fired. I hit dead center on the outline of the man. "When was the last time you shot a firearm?" Officer John asked. "About 6 years ago give or take. Dad used to take us shooting out in the pasture," I replied with a proud smile. Officer John nodded his head, then said, "Take the head shot. Right between the eyes." I repeated the entire routine, breathing and all, and aimed and fired and hit the target right between where his imaginary eyes would have been. "Your Uncle Rex wasn't lying. You kids can shoot. Why didn't you join the force? We could have used someone like you." I looked down a little sheepishly. "Well, for one, I'm extremely small. For two, I was married to a psychopath and wasn't allowed to have a career. For three, it honestly never crossed my mind. I was raised on a farm, guns were used for protecting livestock, chickens, pigs, and family. I never thought about shooting another human unless it came down to someone breaking and entering or trying to hurt my family. I never thought I would *need* to think about defending myself from another human. I guess when you are living with the devil itself, everyone else seems like an empty threat." Officer John looked a little sad, and said, "Well if you ever reconsider. We would be lucky to have you join us when all this is over." I nodded and shook his hand. "Thank you, sir. That means a lot."

We stayed and fired over 100 rounds a piece, even Momma. I think she enjoyed it. It was kind of nice to get back in the feel of being in control. Every piece of control that I took back made me feel sturdier, stronger, and more ready for whatever might be coming my way.

We thanked the officers and assured them we could walk back to Don's just fine. It was just Lane, Momma, and myself, but it was broad daylight, and I didn't think we would be in any immediate danger. The Walkers weren't the smartest, but I didn't think they were dumb enough to come after us in the middle of the day outside a police station. I looped my arm through Lane's and my other arm through Momma's and we made our way back to Don's. We walked in the front door, and it still felt weird not seeing Don standing behind the counter giving me hell. For a minute, my heart sank again, and I just stared. Dad and Uncle Rex came back in from the kitchen area and said it was as good as they were going to be able to get it. Momma then told them that she would find some bleach and go at it again, and she disappeared into the kitchen. I wasn't ready to face it back there, not yet. I just wanted to be in my comfort zone, which was this side of the kitchen.

I took a breath and let it out and asked the guys if they wanted a beer. Of course, they did, so I grabbed enough to go around and passed them out. Dad opened his and sat down with a thud at the bar next to me. He turned to me and said, "About Don. How close were you two?" I looked down at my beer and cupped it in both hands and replied, "Well, Dad. If I couldn't have you, he was about the closest I could get. He died for me, most likely protecting my information from them. They probably wanted my address, which Don knows, and he apparently didn't give it to them, because I'm still in one piece. He was a great man, and he really cared, but was never overbearing about it. He'd give me a hard time, then move on to the next customer. I think he always wanted a family, but just said it wasn't in the cards for him in this life. I'm not sure if that meant he had tried and failed, or if he just chose not to try, but he was always here. Always a friend, from the very first day I showed up." He nodded, like he understood. "I'm glad you had someone like that here to be with you. I'm sad that you needed it, but glad you had it." I looked at him in the eyes and I said, "I know, Dad. They don't make them like Don anymore.  He will be missed for as long as I'm alive, for sure."

We had forgotten to lock the door behind us, and another regular named Sam stumbled in.  It looked like he had started early this morning.  "Hey Sam.  I have some bad news."  I grabbed his regular beer and brought it with me and sat down next to him and handed it to him.  I walked through the scenario and shared some tears with Sam over the story.  "Delaney, he loved you.  You were the highlight of every day for him.  I'm glad you got this place, and I hope you keep it running.  I'll leave ya'll to it for now, but if you need anything, reach out.  Okay?"  I nodded and patted him on the back.  I was getting better at touching people every time I did it.  "Thanks Sam, I appreciate it.  I'll see you soon, okay?"  "Sure thing," Sam said with a nod, and then he headed out the door into the sun which was sinking a little lower than I would have liked.

"Hey guys, I need to go check on Don's house.  I know he had mentioned having a dog a few times, and it's probably starving.  Also, it may be a good place to stay for now, and you could park the RVs in the yard.  Knowing Don, it has a yard.  Let me grab the keys and we can all head that way, okay?"  I went to get the three sets of keys and remembered the Bronco.  "I think I'm going to drive the truck.  Any of you want to ride with me?"  Jace and Luke got up and both said they would go with Lane and I in the truck.  Uncle Rex was going to watch over Momma while she cleaned and Greg, Jamie, and Dad would follow us in the RVs.  We made sure to turn off the sign and lock up behind us, and I left Momma with the spare key to Don's that was on his other keychain.  We made our way around the back of the bar where I figured the Bronco would be parked, and there it was, and it was gorgeous. A 1987 Ford Bronco, black and shiny with red trim, massive tires, and clean wheels, with leather interior and an aftermarket stereo system that we soon found out would blow your hair back. To say that Don had taken care of the truck would be an understatement. He had restored and brought back to life this amazing beast, and I would drive it with pride and take just as much care with it knowing how much he put into it and what it must have meant to him.

We took off down the road and Lane was giving directions from the passenger seat. We finally reached our destination, and it was definitely a destination to want to reach. This house was a two-story old-style Victorian with a wraparound porch, fresh paint, sitting on about 8 acres which was unheard of in this part of Tulsa. It must have been old land that he wasn't willing to split up and sell for his retirement yet. We filed out of the Bronco and walked up the front steps. Right away I heard a little bark and figured Fritz would have a friend now to keep him company while I wandered around instead of being home enough for him. We opened the door to find this little dog that was nothing more than fur. You couldn't see its eyes or make out where it's ears were. It was black and about the size my forearm. It whined when it realized we weren't Don, and then jumped in circles wanting attention. Jace bent down to pick it up and started baby-talking to it, which made us all laugh. We needed the icebreaker and Jace had always been really good at providing those.

We walked into the foyer, which was amazing and massive, with a staircase winding up to the second floor right there in the entrance. The kitchen and dining room were on the left with the living room, den, and an office on the right. There was a half-bath downstairs and the master suite with a master bathroom that blew me away. The tub was big enough to fit 4 people comfortably, and the shower was big enough for about 7 people to stand up in and still have breathing room, and there were two sinks with a huge vanity between them. The entire wall above the vanity was a mirror, but the rest was made from stone tiles. The entire bathroom probably weighed a ton. Upstairs there were 5 more bedrooms, two of which were rather small and probably used as game rooms, libraries, offices or nurseries back when it was built, but the other three were very large. Two had a Jack and Jill bathroom between them and the third had its own bathroom. There was another bathroom between the two smaller bedrooms on the right side of the staircase. The house was enormous, well taken care of, and well lived in. It looked like it belonged in Georgia out in the sticks, but here it sat, in Tulsa, Oklahoma, and it was mine. I wasn't sure what to do with that knowledge, but I did know now that we all had places to sleep as all the bedrooms were completely furnished, even though the smaller rooms just had a twin bed a piece, the larger rooms had queen beds in two of the rooms and a king in the other. There didn't seem to be a speck of dust anywhere. Again, Don surprised the heck out of me. I figured I'd have to investigate this house to see if he inherited it or how this match happened, because I had no idea.

We found food for the pup and read on his collar that his name was Frank. Rather peculiar name for a dog, but in some places, I guess so was Fritz. So now we had a Fritz and a Frank. I called Momma to let her know to stop by the apartment and use my spare key that was under the mat to pick up Fritz before coming out so he could meet his new brother. She said that was no problem. Dad, Greg, and Jamie had parked the RVs in the yard and were literally standing there staring at the house like they weren't sure what to do. I opened the door and invited them in and showed them around.

"D, hun, this is easily a million-dollar house. Maybe more these days, especially with the land. You had no idea he lived here?" I looked at Dad and replied, "No idea. At all. I didn't even know his dog's name other than him calling him *that mutt, or* what the Bronco looked like. He was sitting on a goldmine and working in a bar that used to do well, but now was just a place he probably liked to hang out and visit with people. That probably *was* his retirement. He didn't need to quit, and he had no family, so we became his family. I can't believe he left all of this to me. Why me? Why not Sam or one of the other regulars?" Dad looked thoughtful and then replied, "Well, he apparently knew you needed it. You needed a sturdy place to build your life and find yourself, and this is a place that anyone could do that in. He knew you needed peace and with 8 acres, even in Tulsa you will have peace, even though I'm sure I'll have to drive up and care for this lawn more times than I can count." He smiled a little at that and walked off to go look in the kitchen.

Don always told me I needed a new beginning. A fresh start. Today, on the day he died, he made sure he gave it to me. Most likely his reasoning was that he wasn't sure if anyone else would or could. He gave me a place to plant roots. To grow. To be me and start a life. Possibly even start a life with Lane. This was my next chapter. This was when I gained my control back. This is when the world would smile on me and get me through this last bit of terror, before hopefully setting me loose to enjoy the rest of my days. This was my time. I was going to be thankful for every second of it, even the scary ones.

# Chapter 9

I wasn't ready to go to sleep. I wanted to stay awake and just cherish this time with my family. In a way, I felt like I was honoring Don's memory by doing just that. Jace went and got a case of beer, and everyone chose a room to stay in. I took the main suite, mostly because it was the biggest and had the most room for someone to keep watch over me, though that seemed really strange for me to accept already. I called Dr. Baker and told her we would be moving into Don's house, and gave her the address so she could have the camera setup transferred. She still wanted it on camera even if I was apparently going to have witnesses present in the room with me. She wanted to see with her own eyes what was going on with me in case the stress made the night terrors worse and she needed to intervene. She asked for my family's contact information, and I gave all of the numbers and names over to her.

Uncle Rex was not drinking, as he had decided by himself to be the gatekeeper to the house. He was sitting on the front porch, with a Glock on his hip and a shotgun across his lap. He said if nothing else, it would be a deterrent for anyone that even thought of stopping by that wasn't family. Turned out, he just scared the hell out of the kid that showed up with the camera set. After checking his ID, and asking him some questions, he allowed him to come inside, but told Jace to stay with him. I guess he didn't want to take any chances, no matter what the circumstances were. The kid seemed like he didn't mind, and in the end thought it was cool that there was an old man guarding my house and that the old man had also given him an escort.

The rest of us were sitting at the kitchen table talking about life and how much things had changed. Dad looked at me and said, "Okay, D. Lane and I talked, and he hasn't gotten much sleep the last few nights, so he is going to take one of the small rooms upstairs. Jace and I are going to keep watch over you tonight while you sleep, and if we need backup, we will wake the others. What are the rules of engagement and how do we keep you from hurting yourself or us while you are out?" I laughed at the *rules of engagement* comment. "Well, Dad. The best thing you could do is stay as far away from me as possible and let it run its course. That's really the only way to keep you from getting caught in the crossfire. If you feel like you *have* to engage with me, then be calm, don't try to restrain me, and just talk to me like we are having a conversation and hope that I snap out of it. If I don't, let it run its course." Dad shook his head. "I don't like the thought of sitting there while you hurt yourself. That's going to be extremely hard to watch but waking you up in the middle could cause more harm than good is what your doctor told me. So, we will play it by ear and hope for the best. Jace and I will take shifts with Greg, Luke, Rex, Jamie, and your Momma. We will always keep one person on the door and the other in the room with you. 3-hour shifts so everyone gets sleep. Does that sound good to ya'll?" Everyone nodded in agreement, but I just sat there feeling bad that I was keeping everyone from a full nights sleep. They weren't going to take no for an answer, so I would have to let it be.

I nodded and headed to the big bedroom. Momma had brought me some clothes from the apartment and Lane's bag from my apartment, so Lane followed me in, grabbed his bag, and turned to leave. "Lane, wait." He turned and looked at me with a sad smile on his face. "Yeah?" I walked over to him and gave him a kiss on the cheek. "Just because they are here, doesn't mean I don't need you, okay? Please stick around. Indefinitely. You could get out of your lease and move in if you want. There is plenty of room for you here, and when the family finally leaves you could move into one of the bigger rooms, you know?" He smiled a little bigger. "D, I'm not going anywhere. I'll look and see what I have left on my lease, but let's just get through this first, okay? I want to make sure he is gone, one way or the other. Love you, get some sleep." "Love you too, Lane. Goodnight."

With that, he left me standing there. I closed the door and changed clothes, then opened the door and announced to Jace and Dad that I was going to bed.

Jace dragged a recliner from the living room into the space between the bed and the wall beside my bed and sat down and got comfortable. I was staring at the ceiling trying to put off the tiredness that was creeping into my mind. This day had taken a huge toll on me mentally, and I was again hoping for the best but expecting the worst. I guess for the foreseeable future, we were just going to hope to stay alive. The only difference was for me, I had to stay alive in my dreams and in real life. I closed my eyes and drifted off.

### *The Carnival*

*It was a carnival, but the dead of night. I was all alone and walking through a spread-out little town of sorts. There was a dirt road going through the middle and off to the side there was a downhill slope on both sides with huts that you could walk into to see the different attractions or games. There were dim lights trailing from hut to hut, but not much other light. I had never seen anything quite like it before, but at the same time it felt familiar. The mood with the lighting and location was sinister, but it was welcoming with all the participants at the same time. So many people being there made it seem like it would be a fun place to go through.*

*I was walking down the center and turned to my right and there were a group of kids going into this particular hut, but I never saw any of them come out. I found it strange because none of the huts seemed to have a back door. I decided I should check it out and started the downhill walk to the hut. I walked in, and there was nothing but a big red box in the center of the hut with a lock on it that looked ancient and rusty, even though the box appeared brand new. The box itself was* made of shiny red vinyl with red velvet trim. On close inspection, it was absolutely beautiful. It reminded me of a treasure chest you would see in a gypsy camp back in the days where there were many around. I reached out and touched it just to feel how it felt beneath my fingers.

"Hello?" I asked as I took a closer look around. In the back right-hand corner, the black curtains didn't quite meet and there was a gap big enough to look through without actually moving the curtain. I carefully stepped over to the curtain just close enough to put my eye up to the gap to see what was on the other side, and what I saw left me with more questions than answers. Inside, there were conveyer belts that seemed to be looping and hurtling in every direction and they were all moving and carrying loads of children to a destination that wasn't clear. The walls inside were black and distorted the view just enough to where I couldn't see what exactly was happening. I felt a hand on my shoulder, and I spun around face to face with a man that looked like a walking corpse. His hands were more bone than flesh, and his skin appeared to be hanging from the bone all over his body. He had no hair and looked to be about 80 years old but could have been close to 65. It was hard to tell in the condition that he was in. It looked like he hadn't eaten in a decade.

"You are a little old to be in here, aren't you? What is your purpose?" He inquired in a voice that sounded like sandpaper and breath that smelled like rotten meat. I gestured to the gap in the curtain and spoke. "What are you doing with all the children? Why aren't they awake? Where are they going?" He threw his hands up and down like I was exhausting and irritating him. "That's a lot of questions for a trespasser to ask with no business being in my domain in the first place, now, isn't it? Maybe you should ask yourself why you couldn't leave well enough alone and stay outside? I didn't invite you in, and there is no reason for you to be in here."

The hostility was coming off this man in waves. He wasn't happy to have anyone in his territory, and he wasn't shy about letting me know about it. Those children belonged to someone somewhere and they had to be missed. Why had they come in alone? Where were their parents? Why wasn't there a massive panic outside with childless adults screaming in agony at the loss of their cherished little ones? Where was the outrage? I was outraged, and I didn't know any of the children in that room. I wanted to take all of them away somewhere safe where I knew for sure they were going to be okay. My heart was aching, and I had a gut feeling that this place was anything but your ordinary carnival.

"If you don't answer where these babies came from or why they are knocked out and on conveyer belts headed to God knows where, then I'm going to step out and go find someone to help me figure out the answer." He scoffed and made a snorting sound and came back to meet my eyes. He moved up close to my face and spat out, "Stupid girl, you don't have a clue what you stepped into. These kids are no longer wanted. Nobody wanted them to begin with. I saved them from the clinics where mothers had gone to throw them away like trash. I used them for what I needed them for, which is none of your business, and now they are in hibernation until the next experiment, which is also none of your

123

*business. I wake them up once a week and let them roam and play and be children, but they always come back willingly. They are fed, when necessary, and they are clothed with the necessary clothing that is needed for the weather, and their medical needs are tended to by me. They want and need for nothing; therefore, you are crossing a line by barging in here and trying to take them from me."*

*"What kind of experiments?" I asked the old man. I wasn't sold on the fact that these kids came back to this man willingly. I was a grown adult and wanted to run away. He scoffed. "Again, none of your business. All you need to know is these experiments change lives and make them better for the outside world. Without them, cures would not be found, and lives would be snuffed out before they ever began. Did these kids make a sacrifice? Yes, of course. But they got to live." He was speaking like he was doing these kids a favor and he was saving the world in the process, which I didn't buy into for a moment. "Does the Government know what you are doing here? And what's in the red box?" He scoffed at me again and threw up his hands. This must be something he does a lot, since I had made him do it twice in a matter of a few minutes. "The Government chooses not to know what I'm doing, and the box truly is none of your concern. I understand you are weary about my intentions with these children, but I assure you they are treated with respect and are given a chance whenever necessary to be able to just be children. I'd have it no other way. In the end, the Government accepts the experiment data and the outcomes, and that's all they worry about. Test subjects are not a concern of a government that looks at the big picture, and they are not a concern for me other than*

*keeping them happy and healthy enough to continue
the good work we are doing here. Whether you agree
with the situation or not is of no consequence to me.
You have no rights here, and you need to leave. Now."
He started shooing me toward the door.*

*I gave him a look that would kill him dead if I'd
had such power, which sadly I didn't, and I turned to
make my way out of the hut. I made my way a few huts
down to where a crowd of people my age was scattered
about inside and outside, and I nudged my way through
the initial crowd. I walked into a room with mirrors on
all the walls that was actually bigger than what it had
appeared outside. Everyone was drinking, taking drugs
of various kinds, dancing, smiling, and having a good
time. They were all touching me as I went by, but for
once I didn't mind. I was so disheartened after what I'd
just seen that I'd take the human contact any way I
could get it. I would have rather held all those children
and told them it was going to be okay, but it was too
late for that.*

*I found a guy in the corner with jet black hair,
blue eyes, dressed in all black with his shirt unbuttoned
sitting at a table with a drink in his hand observing the
crowd. His eyes met mine and didn't look away, so I
made my way through the throng of people to his table.
"Are you from here?" I yelled over the blaring music. He
nodded. "You could say that. I've never known
anywhere else. Why do you ask?" I looked down at my
hands and then raised my eyes to match his gaze and
got the courage up to just ask. "Do you know the old
man across the street? What's up with him and the
kids?" His eyes flashed to the dance floor, and they
changed. They hardened and turned to an ash grey as if*

*what he was about to say truly upset him, and he was working hard at putting words together or trying to forget something so he wouldn't have to speak at all. "Most of the people you see here came from there. This is our reward. The town. We stay with Bones until we turn 18. Then we are given a hut, a job, and told we could live freely within the compound, but we can never actually leave the compound. If you look around the room, aside from you, I see only 3 strangers that didn't grow up here and go through Bones. It's just how we live."*

*"You were experimented on?" I asked, trying to judge exactly how terrible or safe these experiments were. He looked at me dead in the eyes and took his shirt off. He had more scars than skin that wasn't scarred starting at his shoulders and going all the way to his wrists. It looked like they had taken biopsies, flesh, done injections, IVs, burned him, frozen parts of him, about anything that the skin could react to had been done to his arms. "My legs look the same as my arms," he said. "He leaves our chests, faces, hands, and feet alone. He said that way at least there is a semblance of perfection left on our bodies, but that is all we get. Nothing more, nothing less. Look around. It has to be 90 degrees in here, and you and the 3 other guests are the only ones in short sleeves or tank tops." I looked around. Sure enough, he was right, we were. The girls were wearing tanks, but they had button up blouses draped over them with sleeves to their wrists. "It's not all bad," he pointed out, "At least we don't have to worry about clothes, food, houses, medicine, or anything else that normal people worry about on a normal basis. We just get to live, party, drink, and have fun for the rest of our lives. Most of us live to be fairly*

*old. Bones originally was one of us, but he got promoted about 30 years ago, before my time. There were stories, though. He truly believes what he is doing is saving the kids, and nobody will convince him differently. There are good jobs to have here, and there are bad jobs to have here, but the biggest job is to look like you are having a blast to keep what little customers we get spending money as long as possible. Hence the party tent with all the best-looking ones of us in attendance every night. Most of the pills are fake, the drinks are real, but if we overdo it and don't show up tomorrow, we get demoted to a tent of the Leader's choosing, which could be anything from serving food to shoveling crap from the animals. We are cared for though; you don't need to worry about those kids. We should never have been born to begin with, so we get the life that we get. That's all. None of us think any more or any less about it. This is just our lives and how it will be from here on. At least we all have each other."*

*I wasn't buying into the fact that they were all happy with their circumstances. "How many of you are there?" He sighed and looked exasperated, "You ask a lot of questions. There are hundreds of us. We do get days off like anyone else, or sick time like anyone else. Obviously, we can't all be working every day all the time. There are shifts, and there are rules we have to abide by, which none of us have a problem with, so I'm not sure why you would have a problem with it. You can leave. We have to stay. This isn't your problem, and I'm honestly not sure why the hell you are still here. You can't save the world, Delaney."*

*I stopped thinking about everything else, and asked, "How did you know my name?" He smiled a* conspiratorial smile. "I know everyone's name that steps into this carnival. I knew you would be an issue and I knew you would have questions, so I made myself readily available for you and even made eye contact, but I think it's time that you left us in peace. Bones got pretty upset with you and he is looking for you as we speak. He doesn't want to use the red box, but he will if he feels you will be trouble or come back with trouble after you leave." I had no idea what he meant as using a box as a threat. "What's in the red box? Why is it locked?" I asked with more urgency as he started shoving me out of the front door of the hut. "The box is a weapon. A weapon we don't like to use but have to use on occasion."

I stepped into the night air and went to turn, but Bones was standing right there blocking my way with 6 men at his side. "I think you will find out what the red box is after all this evening, you stupid girl. You should have left at first warning. All, please escort her to my hut and do it quietly. The children are still hibernating, and we don't want anyone to wake prematurely, plus we have guests that don't need to leave quite yet." Two of the men grabbed my arms on either side and started escorting me back to Bones' hut. I didn't fight and I didn't resist, mostly because I was curious. What was the weapon in the red box, and what could it possibly do to me?

"Sit her in the back," Bones said as he walked to the front of the box and slid in a key that looked like it belonged to a door in a castle in the middle of England that had been forgotten for hundreds of years. They sat me down and opened the box and took out a device that looked like a helmet. They came over to me, put it on my head, and turned it on. It lit up with little lights that lit up my face and blinded me momentarily. It made a wheezing sound like it hadn't had to work in a while and it was protesting, but it came on. Suddenly there was pain, and a lot of it. Blood was rolling down the sides of my face, but the pain was everywhere around my head. Piercing, throbbing, pain.

"You see, child, there are scalpels filed down on both edges to form a sharp tiny double-edged knife embedded in the device. When it is turned on, they are all sent into your skull at about 500 feet per second. There are rods attached to the end which are hooked up to the electric belt within the helmet that focus mostly on short term memory but can erase more if needed. You will not remember us when this is over, but hopefully you will still have motor function and be able to be a productive member of society. It has been over a decade since we have been forced to use the device, so it may have degraded some. There is no safe way to test its abilities without using it. My colleagues here will stay until the process is done and bandage you up, if you are still alive. They will give you a comfortable place to hibernate until you are healed, and then we will drop you at a bus stop in the middle of nowhere. I'd say it was nice meeting you Delaney, but it really wasn't. Good luck."

The machine kept making noise and it felt like there were dozens of probes inside my skull rooting around in my brain. I couldn't move. I wasn't sure if I was too scared to move or if I had lost the ability, but I was betting on the latter. Something that was pierced had taken away my motor function and I was stuck staring at these men that I didn't know and hoping that

*I would live through this. The probing and the pain continued, and I was powerless to stop it. My chest started heaving and I started hyperventilating. I couldn't get enough oxygen. At that point two of the men came over and hooked the helmet to two hooks that were implanted in the wall. They wanted to make sure that if I passed out my head stayed upright and where it was supposed to be for the remainder of the procedure. Tears started streaming down my face, and my eyes had turned to tunnels. Behind the men, I could see the guy from the party hut walking toward me slowly, but the black that was taking over my vision closed in before he reached me. The world went dark.*

*I could hear my breath, but that's all I could hear, and then after what seemed like days, I couldn't even hear that anymore.*

## Chapter 10

I started to wake up and realized I still couldn't move. I opened my eyes to an audience. Mom, Greg, Rex, and Jamie were standing at the foot of the bed looking at me with concern written all over their faces. Lane, Dad, Jace, and Luke were each holding one of my limbs down to the bed. When they realized I was awake, Dad nodded, and all of them let go and straightened up to a standing position. Mom looked nervous and said, "I'll go start some breakfast. D, I'll bring you some coffee from the kitchen." With that, she reached over and lifted my journal off the counter and handed it to me, then turned and walked out of the bedroom door. Lane looked the least surprised and frightened of any of them. I knew my face had to be all sorts of shades of red, but I couldn't find any words. I hadn't seen them in years, and now they see the worst of me within 24 hours. I was horrified and mortified all at once. I wanted to run as far and as fast as I could, but I had to stop running. I had to face this. I had to speak.

"Was it that bad?" I asked with a look on my face that was supposed to look quizzical, but really probably just looked like I wanted to crawl in hole and die. Dad shrugged. "I've wrangled cows, been bucked by horses, caught wild hogs, and fought off coyotes and I will tell you one thing, girl. You have not lost an ounce of strength no matter what you think. You may be small, but you about kicked my butt. I had to run and grab Jace and wake Luke to get the rest of them up to help." He laughed a little like he was just realizing how funny that probably looked on tape. The tiniest one in the family going stark raving mad and taking on a bunch of grown cowboys. That made me grin too, then I started chuckling, then it turned into rolling laughter. Everyone else joined in shortly, and Momma walked in with the coffee with a smile on her face as well. She turned to me, "D, drink your coffee, follow the doc's orders, and write your dream down, and then we need to go to town to check on the progress with the police. On a lighter note, love, I think people back home would pay to see that video." They were trying to make light of the entire situation for my benefit, and I knew it. I also wanted to thank them for it, but I didn't. I just nodded with a grin, took the coffee, and opened the journal and began writing my journey from the night before.

Lane, Mom, Dad, Jace, and I loaded up in the Bronco to head to town. The rest stayed behind to look over the house and come up with a plan. We got to the police station, and I walked in and asked for Officer John Harold. The lady at the desk nodded and said he was in, and she would call for him. We sat and waited in the lobby, and he came out and waved us back about 5 minutes later. We got into his office and there were only two chairs, so the men stood and let Momma and I sit. Officer John looked like he hadn't slept a wink last night.

"Delaney, I need more information on Justin. I hate to ask you, but his family won't speak to us at all, and we need more to go off of if we plan to actually get him in custody. I know this is a sore subject for you, but I need you to tell me about the incident and your life preceding the incident in as much detail as you can remember. I'm going to record this, and we can work forward from there. We need enough background that we can hopefully find him and apprehend him before anything worse happens. Can you concentrate for me and please start at the beginning? If you don't want your family present for this, then they can wait outside." I shook my head. "I spoke to them yesterday and told them everything. They can leave if they want, but I have nothing to hide." He nodded as if he knew this was hard on me but there wasn't another way. "Then please go ahead and begin whenever you are ready."

I started with school, telling him how I didn't think Justin ever knew I existed.  He was popular, had tons of friends, in every sport he could get in, and everyone that was beneath him was invisible, and I was definitely beneath him.  When I graduated, he had shown up to see one of his teammates graduate, and it was like he had seen me for the first time.  He stepped up and started a conversation with me, and I was so surprised and stunned that I fell hard and fast.  We dated for a little over 2 years and he asked me to marry him.  I was 21 when we got married, even though everyone tried to talk me out of it.  I think that somehow made me want to marry him more, like some kind of forbidden thing, and I'd always had a little bit of an issue with people telling me how to live my life.

He moved me to Tulsa and isolated me from everyone after we were wed.  He wouldn't let me be around anyone without him and kept a tight leash on me.  I couldn't even go to the store without permission.  He had a tracker on my phone and knew if I broke the *rules*.  It was a nightmare, then the beatings started, and things just kept getting worse.  I had to go to the hospital a lot, and it got to where they were looking at me out of the side of their eyes.  They knew something was going on, but I had an excuse for every injury, because he would never leave me in the hospital room alone and I was honestly scared of what he would do to me if I had told them the truth.  We lived like that for 5 years.  Same song different tune.  Nothing was ever good enough and I wasn't to be trusted.

The day of the incident, I left without asking him.  I went driving downtown just to see the buildings and see people that didn't fear for their safety every second. The anonymity called to me, so I got out and I sat on a bench for hours. Justin was at work, so I wasn't worried until it got to be 5 in the evening. At that point, I knew he would be out for blood. I'd never disobeyed him like that, and I had never disappeared for almost an entire day without any sort of communication either. Sure enough, he tracked me to the bench where I was sitting using that app on his phone. I saw him pull up, and I figured he couldn't hurt me in public, so I stayed put. Too many people were getting off work and there were too many eyes watching. I thought that if I could just somehow *stay* in public, maybe things would be okay. They weren't okay. He got out smiling ear to ear like he was happy to see me, which was scarier than if he had looked angry. He sat beside me and pressed a gun to my side and told me that I'd better smile back and get into the car without causing a scene or I'd pay for it later, so I complied. I stood up and made my way to his truck and climbed into the passenger seat fighting back the urge to vomit or cry. He made his way slowly around the vehicle, keeping his eyes on me the entire way to be sure I didn't move. He got into the driver's seat and looked over at me with such contempt, I knew I had crossed a line I couldn't come back from.

He backed out of the parking spot, keeping the gun pointed at me. He told me to stay unbuckled and to keep my hands in my lap. He slammed on the breaks and my head got thrown into the dashboard, then he gunned the gas and my head slammed back against the seat in the truck. I could taste the blood and I figured my nose was broken or my lip was busted at the very least, but I felt nothing. I had finally given up fighting back, and I kept my hands in my lap. He turned a sharp left and my head slammed into the window. My hands never left my lap. The gun was still trained on me, and he was enjoying every moment. He had to be seeing red, because he wasn't thinking of all the evidence his own truck was collecting against him. I was mentally preparing to die. I knew that's where this was heading. He was making a mess out of his truck and that was his most prized possession. This was the end of the line for me, and I felt nothing.

I sat in the seat with my head held high, and he hit the brakes again hard, and my head hit all the way at the bottom of the windshield while my body slammed into the dash of the truck then he lurched it forward and my body fell back into the seat hard, but I just resituated and put my hands back into my lap. I wasn't going to let him see how what he was doing was affecting me. I wasn't going to give anything away if I didn't have to. He got onto the highway, and it was starting to get dark as the sun was setting on what I knew would be the last day of my life, but I was going to face it with my head held high knowing he wasn't going to take that from me. I was going to go out, but he wouldn't get to see me lower my head to him again. Never again. When he bored of throwing me around the cab, he set the cruise control on the truck, and reached across and opened the window on my side. He told me to get onto my knees and face the window with my hands still in my lap. I complied again. I didn't have much choice. Then he held the gun to my back and told me to jump out. That's the first time I refused. I didn't say anything, but I just sat there. I wasn't going to kill myself. He wasn't going to get off that easy. If he wanted me dead, he was going to have to do the work. It was like he understood what my defiance in that moment meant, because he hit me at the base of my neck with the butt of the gun and rammed his shoulder into my backside when I leaned forward from the blow. I landed on the shoulder of the highway headfirst, which doctors were surprised didn't break my neck, but I guess I had fallen enough in life that my subconscious took over and saved my life by falling gracefully, or at least as gracefully as one can fall out of a window speeding down the highway. I was in a coma for a few months, and when I woke up, they had already arrested him. "That's all I know," I stated as I looked at the officer. He nodded his head and stopped the recording.

"I had your statement from the incident, but I needed the background with it. I'm sorry to have to put you through that again. His brother Joe, did he play any role in the abuse?" I thought about it for a minute, then recalled, "He tried to help me a few times, or at least pretended to. I really think now that it was just a ploy between Justin and him. Justin didn't want me reaching out to anyone else for help or assistance, so he put Joe in situations when he knew I wanted to get out. He gave me someone that acted kind and listened to me, even though Joe never really did anything about it. To me, it seems like it was all a setup looking back and seeing how Joe is acting now. He never cared about me or my safety. He was probably just doing Justin a favor by playing nice with me to try to keep me quiet and placated."

Officer John nodded sadly and conceded, "I think you are right on that. It appears that Joe and Justin both had friends on the inside and also a few on the outside that made this entire escape possible, and that includes someone on the force. He shouldn't have made it 10 feet nonetheless all the way out of sight when he did what he did. They stood down, and the order came from the radio. I'm still trying to find out who gave the order, and I will find it out, but until I do Delaney, we can't even trust my people. So your protection is me, Roger, and the family you have around you right now. But I promise you I will do everything in my power to keep you safe. I've known Roger my entire life, and he was with me when that call went out, so we can rule him out as a conspirator. I just want to be upfront with you about what we are dealing with. This is bigger than just you, but I think you are what they are after. I know you want to open Don's back up, and I won't stop you, but you keep people with you at all times. Don't even go to the bathroom by yourself, do you understand that?" I nodded. "You still got that gun on you?" He asked. I nodded again. He said, "Keep it close and make sure you never go anywhere without it. Any of you. I have a feeling Justin will want to finish the job himself, but just in case, trust nobody. I'll do what I can from here, and I'll call you all if I have any update."

I stood up feeling defeated and I must have looked defeated because everyone hovered around me like I was fragile. I hated feeling fragile again and I hated that they saw it all over me like a stain. We walked out the front door together and Lane stepped up into stride with me and hooked his arm around my shoulders like he used to when we were kids and were headed off on some adventure around the neighborhood. "D. You didn't tell me all the details before. You didn't go through it all with your family either, I was there. I didn't know he wanted you to do it yourself. You made it sound like he opened the door and just shoved you out." I looked down. "No. I think it would have made him happier if I'd decided to do myself in, because then he could write me off as just another crazy woman. He wouldn't have had to try to explain all the blood in his cab or the bruise in the small of my back from his gun, or the welt at the base of my neck from the butt of the gun, or the fact that I didn't fight back. There was plenty of evidence that it was his doing, and that's why he got arrested while I was still unconscious in the hospital. If I had fought back, he could have claimed self-defense and said that I assaulted him, and he pushed me and that would have been the end of it. He sealed his own fate by telling me to keep my hands in my lap, and I knew it the second he said it. I took the beating, but I wasn't about to jump out of the window. He would have had to shoot me, Lane. And he couldn't afford to go around shooting people that hadn't fought him. Justin could have tried to fake it, I guess. You know, tuned himself up and acted like I did it. But the evidence wasn't there, and he knew it. My hands were clean. My hands were about the only part of me that *wasn't* bruised and beaten. He couldn't have claimed I beat him or even tried to under the circumstances. That was how I got him dead to rights. He knew the minute I flew out the window that it would come back to haunt him. I just don't think he cared enough to change his plans. He was too furious and he didn't think it through to the end."

With that, we walked in silence for a while. He pulled me closer, and I let him. It was comfortable. It was safe. Then, I noticed a car speeding through a stoplight ahead of us. It swerved right as it got to us, and I screamed for the others to run. Lane and I were in front, and it was like it was moving in slow motion. It jumped the curb and I pushed Lane as hard as I could in the direction of the street. Dad had pushed Momma in a similar fashion, and I glanced back at Jace, and he was screaming something at me, but I never heard it. I turned and was staring into the hood of the car, and reflex took over and I jumped and curled into a ball bracing myself for the blow. I hurled into the windshield and heard it break under the force of my body flying across the hood. Everything went black for a second. There was a massive amount of pain and then all I could hear was a horn. I could still hear Jace screaming but I couldn't make out what he was saying. I finally got my eyes to focus and looked to the side of the car. Jace was hurling someone out of the driver's seat, and I saw him hit the guy repetitively. I had never seen the guy before, but from the look of it, he knew who I was, and he definitely knew who Jace was. Dad ran around the side and caught Jace's arm and pulled him off the man.

I was still scared to move. I wasn't sure what all was broken or if I *could* even move. Then it hit me that I didn't see or hear Lane or Momma. I moved my neck and it seemed to work okay, and I was searching with my eyes everywhere for them. Lane was crawling back to the curb and looked like he had the wind knocked out of him. Momma was still laying on the ground, but she looked like she was coherent and okay. Dad pulled the man up on his feet and faced him toward the car. He pulled zip ties from his own pocket that I didn't know he had, and he zip tied the man's hands together like makeshift cuffs. He called out to Momma to call Officer John and Momma sat up and started dialing. I stayed where I was, mostly because I think I had gone into shock and I wasn't sure what was happening, but I knew all my people were safe. All my people were alive and talking, and I was the only one possibly badly injured, which was the best-case scenario. I had gotten them into this mess, and by God I wasn't going to let them die for me. Not a one of them, if I could help it.

Shortly after, I heard sirens and Lane was at my side holding his left ribs like they hurt. I focused hard and I could hear him saying, "They are coming, D. Help is coming. You have to stay with me. Can you tell me what day it is?" I laughed, started coughing, and realized blood was coming from my mouth. I tried to wipe it away so he wouldn't see, but it was too late. He saw and his face had gone white. I didn't know how bad I was hurt, but I wasn't going to focus on that. I was going to focus on Lane's face. Dad's face came into view behind him, and I saw that Jace was keeping the handcuffed man steady against the car with his hip in the guy's backside. I looked at Dad and Lane and I said, "Guys, I'm okay. It's all good. It's all going to be okay. Dad, can you get my phone and call Dr. Baker? Let her know what hospital they take me to? Lane, does it look like anything is broken? I'm still scared to move just in case." My voice sounded weak and strained, but I did my best to project strength. Dad took my phone and walked back a few steps. Lane looked me over like he was examining me for a modeling audition. He kept touching me in random places and asked if it hurt. I didn't have the heart to tell them that all of them hurt, so I faked it and smiled and said some of them weren't as bad. It seemed to make him feel better at the time.

The ambulance pulled up right next to the car. Paramedics started rambling off questions and I heard my dad answering from behind me. I couldn't really pay attention very well, either the shock was still going, or it was wearing off and things were starting to get real. I wasn't sure what exactly was going on, I just knew it was probably bad. I saw Officers John and Roger pull up in their car and rush over to the guy that was at the wheel. They looked at Dad and Jace with a *thank you* gesture, and Officer Roger took the guy to the back of the police car and called another ambulance to make sure the man wasn't injured to cover his hide.

They put me on a stretcher after they secured my neck in a neck brace. I was fine until they stretched me out, and that's when the pain escalated. I screamed, and they were feeling around to see what was broken and what wasn't. The paramedic looked at me and said calmly, "Hello Delaney, we are going to have to sedate you and transport you to the hospital. I want you to know that you are in good hands and most of all that you are safe. Officer John and your friend Lane are going to ride with us to be sure, okay? They made us aware of your situation, and I promise you, I will get you to the hospital safely and we will get you taken care of. Is that okay with you?" I vomited everywhere at the end of his last sentence. There was a lot of blood and I started to get light-headed. He hooked an IV up and put a syringe up to the IV and injected something into it that made me feel like I was hot everywhere. He started counting and I wasn't sure what was going on, and then everything started fading to black.

### *The War*

*I was living in the city. Lane and I had a house that butted up to the downtown area. It was an older house, but sturdy. Two floors, but on the second floor it had a balcony that came out onto the roof from a door in one of the upstairs bedrooms. We had three dogs,*

*Fritz, Bella, and Ama. We were happy and relaxed drinking coffee on the balcony watching the downtown crowds and traffic wind down for the night and the sun relax lower in the sky in the horizon. We were talking about life and how we had come so far, and that's when we saw it.*

*This object that looked like machinery off a space shuttle came soaring down from the sky. We thought at first that it was a piece of a space station that had fallen off, but that didn't stop the panic welling up in my chest that this was something more. We watched it fall through the atmosphere and Lane and I both ran inside, downstairs, and out the front door and towards downtown. Whatever it was would land in a matter of seconds and there were going to be casualties. There were going to be people that needed help. We got almost to 5th street. We were running down the middle of the road, because all the vehicles had stopped to stare into the sky and formed a roadblock. Everyone was unsure which way they should go given the circumstances. Then it hit.*

*When it first made contact there was a blow that shook the earth below our feet, then this cloud went straight up into a mushroom and the power of the blow came back down with the mushroom and fanned out about two blocks. When the force hit the ground again it brought everything that it touched crashing down and then floating up into the sky. I saw people smashed into the ground and then pulled up into the sky like they were levitating, and then once they hit the top of the mushroom, they smashed back down to the ground below. I had never seen anything like it. Limbs were flying away from bodies, cars that were floated in the air and crashed down had landed on groups of people. I had never seen anything with the force that this object had when it had hit the surface.*

*We heard screams as people were trapped in cars, and moans from people that were still alive on the ground. Lane and I split up to go check on different people and set up whatever kind of triage we could do. There was a drug store on the side of the road, and I ran in to ask them if they could bring out all the supplies that they had that we could use to bandage people with or medicines to give them for pain, burns, and the like. The drug store clerk was flushed and said he would have to call his boss for approval, and I yelled at him that we didn't have time for that, and the phone lines were most likely down. It was a matter of life and death, and he could file insurance on it later, but he needed to hurry. With that, he took a cart used for stocking and started loading it with bandages, wraps, burn ointments, antibiotic ointments, pain relievers from over the counter, tape, anything that he saw that he thought would prove useful to us.*

*I went back outside and found some people that didn't look to be in terrible shape. I helped them over to the other side of the road and laid them on the grass and told them to stay where they were. I yelled to Lane to take the worst cases closest to the drug store, and the cases that didn't look to be fatal over to the other side of the road on the grass. I asked the clerk when he came out of the drug store if he sold blankets or towels of any kind. He assured me he did, and I told him to go back in and fill up another basket with all the blankets and towels he could find. It wasn't cold, but there was a chill in the air and these people had lost massive*

143

*amounts of blood. I also told him if he had anything we could use as a tourniquet to bring it out as well.*

*I kept removing people from wrecked cars and sorting them from best case to worst case. The pharmacist from the drug store came out and started assisting me. Soon I had about 20 people that had been working in the stores a couple blocks out running up and asking how they could help. For some reason, no first responders had shown up yet. I tried my cell phone, but still got a busy signal. I dialed 911 anyway, and it pushed through. I got a recording that said it if was in regard to the explosion that just happened, that I needed to stay put and wait for assistance. They weren't taking any more calls at this time. How could 911 leave a voicemail for us in a time like this? How did that even work? Then I did some calculations in my mind, and realized that the police department, main firehouse, and 911 dispatch center had all been in the direct line of the explosion. There was nothing left from what I could tell at this distance. It had leveled everything. Someone had probably remotely patched in the 911 dispatch center and left the voicemail for people calling in and getting rerouted to out of town centers. The police that had been on duty started slowly showing up and making a perimeter. EMTs started showing up as well. Still no firemen, but it had only been about 10 minutes since the explosion happened.*

*I flagged down an officer and an EMT and told them what I had started. They asked if Lane or I had any training and seemed impressed by the system so far. I told him I had taken CPR certification, but no official training. I just knew things had to get done or these people would die. We were outnumbered 30 to 1 with people that were harmed and still alive. He told me to keep doing what I was doing, and the EMT said he would go see to the people that had the possibly fatal wounds in front of the drug store if I could help triage the others and keep bringing people out to safety.*

*The entire downtown area looked like a warzone. There was a fog in the air, that I expected wasn't fog at all but dust and other particles from the explosion. I wrapped a bandana around my face from the drugstore and ran one to Lane to put on as well. I gave him a handful to give to the people with less fatal injuries on the grass and took off to find more injured. A car had fallen back down from the sky upside down and had trapped a family inside. The father was screaming about his daughter in the back seat. I looked in the back seat and checked for a pulse. She was still alive. I used my knife to cut her seat restraints from her car seat and carefully lower her to the ground outside the car. I assured him she was still alive and then cut him out as well. His wife had passed already. There were no signs of life, no pulse, and her eyes were wide open with fear forever frozen on her once beautiful face.*

*We attended to the wreckage for hours. More crews showed up, some professional, some just wanting to do what they could to help. The physical exertion alone was wearing us out. One of the people that owned a restaurant a few blocks away that still had water brought out to go packages of food for all the workers and all the injured that could eat along with bottles and cups of water. I brushed mine off and told him to get it to the injured first, but he insisted I eat. He turned to me with a look of bewilderment and said, "Most of the people you see here would still be trapped if it weren't for you. I saw you and that man running by my place seconds after the explosion happened, even before the second drop of bodies. You need to eat, or you will be of no help to these people, and everyone needs the help right now. Eat. Drink the water. Then get back to work, okay?" I nodded and shoved what food I could in my mouth as fast as possible, then chugged the water as I was taking off to find more people.*

*Lane and I had worked our way to the center of the wreckage about 6 hours after we started. There was no way this was just a satellite piece that had broken off. The government had ways of fixing those issues before they made it to the ground. Blowing them up, disintegrating them, I'm not sure how but I knew there were protocols in place. Why had nobody done that this time? Thousands of lives had been snuffed out in what couldn't have been more than 2 minutes from us gaining the visual to the impact. There is no way this should have happened. Was it a piece of machinery? Or was it a bomb? What had happened and why did nobody have the answers?*

*I crumpled on the ground, held my head in my hands, and cried. It was a like a dam broke and I couldn't stop it. Lane crouched beside me and held me in his arms and just let me sob. I think he was proud I had kept it in this long. There were no bodies for at least a couple of city blocks, but not only were there no bodies, there were no buildings, no sidewalks, no road, just a crater about 40 feet deep at least. Whether it was a bomb or not, whatever had hit the ground had exploded on impact. I got myself together and Lane and*

*I stood up. I had to help, and we had too much to do for me to sit there and let myself go. Not yet.*

*Lane and I returned to the triage points and assisted the EMTs and police where we could. When it came time to transport to hospitals, we were told most of the hospitals were filling up too fast. They had set up tents outside the hospitals and called in every available nurse, doctor, tech, and civilian to assist with the tents. The EMT pointed us in the direction of the first tent setup and asked us if we could start assisting with transport. We both nodded and went to work. We were using blankets underneath the wounded and carrying them to the checkpoints. It was a lot of work, and hard work. Lane nor I were very big, but somehow in situations like this, you find the strength you need to do what you have to do. For the critically wounded there were people racing towards them from the checkpoint with wheelchairs taken from the hospital and other hospice centers. We worked past them with our person on the blanket, made it to the checkpoint, took the blanket back with us just in case the next victim didn't have one, and repeated the process. All in all, Lane and I carried 17 people out of the wreckage before we were told to sit down by an EMT and get evaluated.*

*I honestly had no idea I had been injured. I think adrenaline was pumping so hard for both of us, that we didn't see when we had gotten hurt along the way. To be honest, I couldn't recall what had caused the injuries. We had walked up to the wreckage without so much as a scratch, but I had several open bleeding gashes on my arms and a few on my legs. I'm assuming it was from wrenching on cars and walking through debris. I had never felt the impact though. I had assumed the blood*

147

*all over me was from someone we had carried or assisted.  The EMT sat us down, stitched us up, added butterfly bandages on top of the stitches, then wrapped them in waterproof gauze.*

*A nurse was screaming about how they didn't have enough blood for the injured.  Lane and I offered to assist and told her our blood types.  There was a degree of uncertainty about us giving because our blood could have mixed with just about any of the injured people's blood.  Under normal circumstances, they wouldn't take us, but under these conditions they had a waiver form and if the patient signed it, we could give.  All the patients were signing them.  I think they realized it was just about their only hope if they needed the blood.  They took twice the amount they were supposed to at one time from Lane and I both, thanked us, and told us we needed to rest.  Rest wasn't in the cards just yet, and I have always been stubborn, so we took off walking the wide path all the way around to the other side of the wreckage.  People had already been triaged, so we took wheelchair duty and got 12 more victims to a checkpoint on the other side.*

*It was 5 o'clock in the morning when we decided to call it and head back home and try to find some news.  Our phones hadn't worked to call or search the internet since the incident had happened.  We got home, fed the dogs, and Lane and I showered and cleaned up the best we could.  We were lucky we still had water; we were worried it would have been shut off due to the impact.  We piled onto the couch with the dogs and turned the tv on.  We just had basic cable, as we never really watched it, but the news was on, and it wasn't good.*

*A country south of China that I had never heard of decided to declare war on us. We hadn't been watching the country, because it was so small nobody thought to put it on the radar, but they had a contract with Russia and had used one of its missiles to fire at us. They had more and Russia and China seeing the damage, decided to pile in with the little guy and come after us as well. The United States had taken 1700 hits in the last 12 hours. 1700 cities have been hit and over 9.5 million casualties so far. The news itself was being broadcast from a basement somewhere in Oklahoma City. Everyone had taken cover, just in case. It wasn't looking good that we would win this one.*

*Oklahoma City and Tulsa both had been hit and hit hard. Supplies were running low, hospitals were overrun, people were searching for loved ones, and nobody had any real answers. I still couldn't get a call out to tell my parents and brothers I was okay, and Lane couldn't get his mom on the phone either. We were stuck. I wondered if maybe the pay phones would work that were still working in the underground bank a few blocks over, so Lane and I took off to walk there to check them.*

*There was a line at the payphones, but when everyone saw us, they parted and stared at us like we were famous or something. Someone had apparently videoed the scene right after it had happened. All these people had seen us fighting to save the people and running to assist in triage. The man at the front of the line spoke, "You two get up here and call who you need to. The lines still work. Thank you for what you did today. I saw you carry my granddaughter and son to safety after you cut them free from their car. Most, if* not all of us standing here, saw you save someone we loved. Thank you for doing that when we couldn't. The lady on the other phone backed up and allowed Lane to get up to call his mom, while the man gestured for me to take his place to call my parents. The dial tone started up, I inserted money, then called my parent's home number.

The phone rang for what seemed like forever, then my mom's worried voice answered with a quick and weary hello. "Mom, it's D. I'm okay. Lane is with me. Have you been watching the news?" I could hear her crying on the other end, but she got it together and said, "Sweetheart, we have been watching you since it started. You got hurt, are you okay? Is Lane okay? Can you get out of town and come down here away from the city?" Tears were rolling down my face, but I answered, "No, Mom. I think ya'll need to come up here to the airport. We need to get out. I have a friend who is a pilot. I think he can get us out of the country without passports. We can get asylum somewhere. The news said Ireland, Israel, Italy, and a few other places were taking people that were fleeing. We need to get out and we need to get out now. Pack a bag and get to our house. We will talk more there. All of you." She faltered a little and then said, "I'll get your dad to pack us up right now. We will get there as soon as we can. The roads are all jammed with people trying to get out of the city but getting into the city might be easier. We will just have to work our way around." I sighed and tears started flowing down my cheeks. "Be careful and be fast. Only bring essentials. We can figure out what we need to once we land. Get here now, okay? And Mom?" I asked. I could hear her sobbing and yelling orders at Dad telling him to call the boys. "Yeah,

Delaney?" I sighed again and said, "I love you. Be fast, be careful, and keep an eye on the sky as you are coming in." She said, "Love you, D. We will be there as soon as we can." With that, I hung up the phone.

I don't know what came over me, but I turned to the man behind me in line and I latched onto him in the biggest hug and started sobbing. He held me there and then the others joined in from all around, giving up their places in line. The crowd of people were just holding me there and letting me cry it out. I pulled away, thanked them all, and the man said, "You two are heroes. I hope you are able to get out, I truly do. But, let me say, this place won't be the same without people like you here to protect it." I nodded at the man, and I stepped back to wait on Lane.

Lane's mom was staying close by so she said she would probably beat us back to the house after he finally got through to her. I told him that we needed to make a stop and see if Chris was home. He nodded. We had talked this over on the way to the phone booth, and Chris was really our only option of getting out of here alive at this point if it came to a full-blown war. He was one of my oldest friends, and we hadn't talked in years, but I knew he would do what he could to get us out.

We got to Chris's house, and he swung the door open before we even got to the front steps. He ran out and hugged Lane and I both for a good couple of minutes. He backed up and led us into the house where his wife and kids were watching the news. Lane and I saw our faces for the first time. It was a different channel than we had watched at our house. I saw my face laser focused and running around doing everything I could to find and help people. Now I know what the *guy had seen when he talked about us at the phone booths. Lane and I looked like we had choreographed the moves we were making. We worked together without any break in stride. I turned to Chris and said, "We need to get out of the country, Chris. Can you make that happen? We aren't safe here." Chris shook his head, "Delaney, they have ordered all flights grounded. There isn't an airport in America right now that is allowed to fly. I think they are preparing to shoot down anything in the sky in hopes to catch it before it hits us. There is no way out. There is something I can do, though. I have a friend in Arizona, in the mountains, and he said he would take my family in as well as any friends that needed a place to lay low outside the city. It's a long drive, but it would be well away from any big city population and it's in the mountains, which doesn't seem to be a target at all. They hit Denver, but Denver is a massive tourist attraction, along with Colorado Springs in Colorado, but they only hit Phoenix in Arizona. I think they are wanting to weed out the population, not destroy all of America. If they take us over, they are going to need to be able to use the land."*

*Chris had a point there. Fleeing the country might not work but fleeing the city into the mountains may work just as well, if not better. "Does he have room for my family and Lane's Mom?" Chris smiled, "D, he bought a ghost town up there. He has an entire town that he charges admission to. Plenty of houses, running water and well water, heat, and plenty of animals to hunt and cook. We were going to leave tomorrow morning to head that way if we can find gas." I nodded. "I just filled my tank up and we filled Lane's up yesterday. We can siphon his gas out of his little car and take my bigger car and take the gas with us. We should be able to fit everything we need in there. Hopefully someone will have gas along the way."*

*"Sounds like a plan. Let's meet at the gas station off 146<sup>th</sup> headed out of town tomorrow at noon. Your family should have made it by then." We hugged and Lane and I turned to leave. The walk home was one with more purpose. We had a destination, and we were going to be as safe as we could possibly be given the circumstances. That's really all that we could hope for right now. One day at a time was going to get us where we needed to go.*

*We got home and packed up clothes, dog food, dog toys and supplies they needed, medicines, toiletries, and some food so we wouldn't have to stop. I loaded up the car and we waited. I decided we needed to rest for a bit, and the family would wake us up when they arrived. Both of our mothers had house keys. I was concerned that Lane's mother wasn't there yet, but figured she was still packing and hoped for the best.*

*She showed up about 30 minutes later with a bag packed and concern all over her face. She grabbed both of us into a huge hug and stepped back to assess how badly we were injured, which wasn't bad. It was a little over 3 hours later when my family showed up. They had come in the SUV and Dad had packed extra gas on the back of it for the trip that he hadn't had to use. They sat in the living room, and we told them the plan. Dad seemed to think they would do just as well back home, but he wasn't going to argue over it. He wanted to be with us, and he knew we were set on where we were going.*

We loaded up the cars and followed Chris as he headed west with Lane's mom riding with us and the three dogs, and my parents and brothers following behind us. The highways looked barren. Like nobody wanted to be on the road and everyone was hunching down in place and praying for the best. We made our way through New Mexico with only one stop to use the restroom and fill up at a gas station out in the middle of nowhere. We were all surprised they were open, but the guy acted like it was just any other day. As we turned to leave, he said, "Good luck getting to wherever you are headed to. Godspeed. The world is going to hell." Mom looked at him with concern and said, "Sweetheart, do you have anywhere you can go to? Anyone you can be with?" He looked at her with sad eyes and said, "Ma'am I lost my wife 5 years ago and my son with her. Bad accident out on the highway. I've been waiting to die since that day. I have nowhere I'd rather be than with them. Thank you for asking though. I really do wish you all luck. Stay safe." Nothing more was said, Mom just nodded a final nod and raised her hand to wave goodbye.

We crossed into Arizona and made our way into the mountains in the Northeast region. A gradual glow started forming on the road. There were no streetlights, and we didn't have a sunroof, so I asked Lane to pull off to the side of the road. Chris saw us pulling over from in front, so he pulled off as well and Mom and Dad followed suit behind us. We opened the doors and got out of the cars. We looked up at the sky and the glow was getting brighter and closer. It was so close that we couldn't see which direction it was coming from. It was way bigger than the one we had seen in Tulsa. The mountain was right in front in front of us, and the glow *was now engulfing the entire range. It looked like daylight in the middle of the night.*

*The light got so bright that we shielded our eyes, but there was nowhere to run to, no point in running, because as far as we could see was lit up and the perimeter was just getting larger by the second. My family came up and crowded us from behind and we all huddled together. Tears started flowing. My Dad and Lane held my mother and I and we waited. The explosion happened and the mountain disappeared. It was about 2 seconds later that the wave of power hit us. I flew through the air and landed somewhere all alone. It felt like all of the bones inside my body were crushed. My limbs wouldn't move, and I couldn't catch a breath or see anything. The world was black and there was a ringing in my ears that was disorienting. I just sank into the background and disappeared.*

# Chapter 11

I woke to the sound of machines in my hospital room and realized that I was strapped to the bed. This would be the second night terror where I was restrained and couldn't hurt myself. Normally, that would mean I would have less bruises and contusions, but in this case, I had many more. Dr. Baker was in the room staring at machines on my left, and everyone else was sitting around in different places in the room. Lane had a sling on his arm and was sitting in the window looking out with an expression on his face somewhere between fear and anger. Officer John Harold was sitting at the foot of my bed looking at a tablet. Mom glanced over and noticed I was awake and spoke to me. "Hey D. How are you feeling honey?" I didn't really know how to answer her just yet, so I replied, "Can we take these things off my wrists and feet please?" Mom nodded quickly, and Dad joined her in unstrapping me from the bed. My journal was sitting beside the bed with a pen on it.

Dr. Baker looked over at me, then grabbed the journal and the pen from the small table and laid it on my lap. "Do you need us to leave to write it down? After you write it down, we will go through what all happened and next steps, but I really think you need to stay on top of the journal." She said it like a suggestion, which wasn't common for her. Normally it was more of an order made to sound like a suggestion, but I think she knew we were on different ground now. I nodded and everyone filed out of the room to give me privacy except Lane. He looked at me and shook his head as if to say he wasn't leaving my side ever again, and then just looked back out the window. I didn't fight him on it. I knew I was going to catch grief from him for pushing him out of the way. He would say it wasn't my job to protect him, but his to protect me. Which in my mind, it was reversed. That had always been an issue with us, but I figure if I put him first and he puts me first, we would still turn out to be okay. We were both going to have to get over it.

I finished writing it, and as soon as I was done, I worked hard at forgetting it. I had bigger things to worry about than my night terrors right now. I had almost been killed, and I think that realization was finally dawning on me. I looked at Lane and said, "Can you please get Dr. Baker, so I can see when she is going to release me again?" He turned and stared at me for a moment, then spoke in a scolding tone. "D. You almost died. You pushed me and your dad pushed your mom out of the way while Jace ran right for the driver. You aren't James Bond. You don't get to be the hero in this one, you have got to stay alive. You have got to live. You have a house, two dogs, your entire family, and last but not least, you have me. You can't just leave me here, not after coming back into my life. If you *have* to fight, then please fight. If you don't? Then get out of the way and leave the fighting to someone else. I need you to stick around. Do you understand me?" I smiled and nodded. I did understand him. I felt the same way about him. This was my fight, not Lane's. It wasn't fair that he was even in this position, and he only was in it because I brought him into it. It wouldn't matter if I told him to walk away, he wouldn't listen. He'd still be here, and Momma would have my head for pushing away the first good thing to happen to me in years.

"Hey, Lane?" He turned to look at me again with tears welling up in his eyes. "Yeah?" I patted the bed beside me, and he came over and sat down. I took his hand in mine and looked into his eyes. "I love you. I'm pretty sure I've always loved you. I just never thought too much about it because I knew you my entire life. You were always there. You were a constant everyday connection. I never thought too much about it until I didn't have you. You can be as mad as you want and hold it against me as long as you want. But I won't let you die for me if I can keep it from happening. I need you too much, and this wasn't your problem until I became your problem. Cut me a little slack, okay? I feel better when you are by my side and *not* mad at me, though. So could you maybe get over it pretty quickly so we can come up with a plan to save us all?" He grinned a little and shrugged his shoulders. "You are going to have a lot to make up for after all this is said and done. I'll just start a list." Then we both laughed, and he got up to go get Dr. Baker.

Dr. Baker walked in with a big manila envelope that looked heavy with my family trailing after her. "Is it okay that I share your medical information with everyone present in this room?" I nodded yes, and she gave me a form to sign that had all their names listed on it. I signed it and handed it back to her. "You are probably not in a whole lot of pain now due to the morphine drip I have set up right now. I can prescribe some painkillers, but if you are on them, I'm going to need you to not have the gun on you. So, gauge your pain whenever we take you off them and make a choice. I can't in good conscious have you running around, armed, with a stomach full of substances that can slow your reflexes. That being said, here are the scans." She put the film on the white light-up board on the wall so we could all see the damage. "You have 2 broken rips that we have taped up to keep them from moving as they heal. Your left shoulder was dislocated, but we put it back in place and you will need to use a sling for a week or so. You can use it lightly, but I don't recommend letting it just hang. It could heal wrong and could cause you issues down the road. Please use the sling. You have bruising over most of the left side of your body from landing against the glass of the windshield along with lacerations resulting in 86 stitches up and down your left side. Your hip is bruised and fractured, but I don't think it's a major concern among the other damage. We will keep an eye on it. You had massive internal bleeding and had to have a blood transfusion. Your lung was nicked by one of the broken ribs, but we got that patched up and everything seems to be working okay. You have a concussion, and you will need to be monitored while you sleep, but we already have that covered with the cameras and with your family. I would like to release you, against my better judgement, because it was all over the radio which hospital you were sent to and that your condition was questionable. I don't want anyone gaining access here and trying to hurt you. Now, I'm going to let Officer John let you know what they are doing about the man that did this to you."

"Hey Delaney," Officer John said with a smile that didn't meet his eyes. "The man that hit you was the cellmate of Justin. He had a picture of you and your entire family, including Lane, and was told that all the others were expendable, but you were not to be killed. He wanted you hurt badly and scared, but not dead. Roger and I believe he wants to do that part himself. The orders were to hurt you, then take you to a location where Justin would meet him and take you from him. The guy's name is Blane. He told us everything in turn for a shorter sentence for his 3rd stent in prison. The DA was happy to oblige given the situation and that we needed the information for evidence. All the evidence from the accident and leading up to the accident have been backed up and the originals are kept in a safe in the DA's office due to the situation with the evidence disappearing for your earlier case on Justin. An APB went out first thing after the DA cleared the warrant, and Justin is to be apprehended on-site as an armed and dangerous suspect in attempted murder, assault, harassing a witness, and conspiracy to commit kidnapping, but that's just a start. I want the DA to throw the book at him, and the DA is on board to do just that. When we catch him, and we will, he will never see the light of day again if I can help it." With that, he stepped back and stood there with his hands in front of him like he was at attention waiting for an order.

I turned to Dr. Baker first. "Doc, I don't want the painkillers. I have to deal with all of this with as clear of a head as I can have. I'll go get some anti-inflammatories at the pharmacy after we leave. Can I try to stand up and see if I can walk by myself?" Dr. Baker shook her head slightly, then gave me the approval to stand with assistance. Lane came over and took my good arm and my hand in his and assisted me in standing up. I could stand so I nodded at him to drop my arm and then I took a few steps. My body hurt, even with the morphine, so I knew I was going to regret the decision to not take the painkillers, but I wanted to be clear to think. Everything worked, one foot after the other I made my way across the room and out into the hall. I looked left and caught a glimpse of a man ducking into a hallway. It looked like Joe, but I had barely gotten a glance at him. I started walking that direction out of curiosity and I had the entire family walking about 5 feet behind me. None of them knew what I was doing, but I had to be sure what I had seen. I was dragging my IV stand with me and walking slowly, but I wasn't about to let him get away if he had actually shown up to the hospital. I got to the hallway and turned right and Joe was there. Right in front of me. He pulled a knife and stuck it straight out and pushed the tip of it into my stomach. "Keep walking like nothing is happening and tell your family and the cop to back off." I knew none of that was going to work, but I made a show of letting him think it would.

I kept moving forward and glanced down and there was a little blood where the blade was starting to get through skin under my gown. I nodded and turned and looked stonily over my shoulder. "Hey guys, stay back, okay?" Joe glanced at them all nervously and I just prayed to myself that Lane would go grab Dr. Baker and Officer John and not try to be a hero. They all stopped walking and I kept moving forward with Joe and the knife in my side. We got to the next corner, and he turned left and backed me into the wall. He pulled out the IV and blood started running down my arm. He pushed the IV stand against the wall, grabbed my arm, and took off halfway dragging me down the hallway to the stairs.

I turned to him with fire in my eyes. "You didn't plan very well, did you? How do you expect to get me out of this hospital as slow as I am before anyone gets to you? How well do you think that's going to work out for you, Joe? Huh? You think they are just going to let you stroll out of here with a hostage? That's not how things work." He said nothing just kept pushing me further down the stairs. We had come from the 6$^{th}$ floor, and I was getting slower and slower by the second. The pain was coming in waves, and I was fighting to keep from throwing up from both rage and the dizziness from the concussion. "Joe, you are going to have to give me a minute, okay?  Unless you want to end up having to carry me, give me a minute to breathe."

I stalled on the left side of the top of the 4th floor landing.  I gripped the handrail hard with my bad hand just to give me something to squeeze to try to clear my mind.  I had no resources and no weapon.  I didn't even have any real clothes or shoes, just the hospital socks with little no-slide circles on the bottom.  He looked at me impatiently and went to pull my good arm to drag me down the stairs.  I brought my bad arm back and knew I would regret it the second I did it, but I punched him left-handed right in the throat.  His hands instinctively went up to where I had made impact and he started choking.  I took that second and made a decision.  It was my life or his life, and I wasn't going to die today.  Not in a hospital gown and socks in a stairwell.  This wasn't where my story ended.  I pushed him with both arms fast and square in the chest.  He teetered for a moment then fell backwards.  He landed flat on his back on the staircase and then kept toppling down as gravity did most of the work for me.  I turned and moved as fast as I could through the 4th floor landing door and screamed for help.

Security rounded the corner and I very quickly explained what I did.  A nurse was with them and took me by the arm and took me into an unoccupied room and sat me on the bed and started seeing to my arm and my stomach where the knife had made a superficial cut alongside the dozens of other lacerations on my side.  The security guards came in shortly after and asked if I could step outside and ID the man that had taken me, and I nodded and stood.  I walked out the door and they had Joe strapped to a gurney and he was still alive, and he was livid. It looked like either one of them had busted his nose open or the stairs did the job for them. I nodded and told them that was the right guy, and let them know that my family was aware that I had been taken, and that my family was on the 6th floor. The nurse told Security that she would call them and get me back up to 6 as soon as possible.

I turned to the nurse. "Do you all keep extra scrubs around in case people forget them or need a clean pair?" She nodded and concluded, "They are in the storeroom a couple of doors down. Why?" I started walking the direction she had indicated and found the storeroom and entered. "I'm going to change into scrubs. If Joe is here, then Justin isn't far behind him. I'm a sitting duck in a gown without shoes." The nurse looked down at her sneakers and held her finger to indicate she would be just a minute and walked out of the door. I changed quickly into the smallest size I could find which were still way too large on me, but cinched up at the waist, they would suffice. The nurse walked back in with a pair of grey sneakers with blue trim on them that were my size. She handed them to me and I put them on. She turned to me with concern on her face and said, "They told us all what was going on. The hospital was on high alert and he should never have made it through the doors. With him inside, they will lock us down until they know for sure there are no more threats in the building. I'll walk you to the elevators and see to it myself that you make it back to your family." I nodded a thank you and she took me by the arm and showed me the way to the elevators that would take us back to 6th floor.

When the doors opened there were a half-dozen police officers already there including John and Roger. My family and Lane were standing behind them and pacing around like they wanted to leave. Jace looked up and saw my face and barreled through the officers to get to me. When he reached me, he pulled me in and hugged me hard without thinking of the consequences. I let him hug me and held my breath through the pain. When he let me go, I could see realization hit his face and he winced. "D, I'm so sorry. I wasn't thinking. I was just so scared. I rushed down to the first floor through the staircase on the far side and I was waiting at the bottom. He wasn't getting out of here with you. I promise you that." I looked up at him gratefully and shrugged which sent a jolt of pain down my left side. "Thanks, Jace. Dad already told you, though. I'm tougher than you." I laughed which caused more pain but was worth it. Jace snickered and carefully grabbed my arm and assisted me over to the group. Officer John motioned for us all to make our way to the waiting room at the far corner of the floor, so we huddled together and followed him. Lane looked like someone had hit him in the gut and he was trying to recover. I hated to think what all of this was doing to him. I just wanted it to end, but Justin could only have so many friends and family that would be willing to assist in something like this. He had to be getting desperate and desperate people tended to do stupid things, like sending their brother to kidnap someone at the hospital with police on watch.

Officer John got in front of the group and motioned for everyone to sit down. Lane went to the coffee station in the corner and poured a cup for himself, Mom, and me and brought them over to us on a little tray he had found on the counter. I took mine with both hands and tipped it up to take a drink. It was hot and actually pretty good for a hospital, so I took my time with it. Officer John started speaking. "I think it goes without saying that this is a high alert situation. Either Roger or I will be with the Jameson's at all times. Lee will be assigned with me and Damien you are assigned with Roger. Delaney is to be in sight at all times by at least one person, preferably us unless she is doing something private, then her mother or Lane can take over. We need this man apprehended yesterday, and my captain has put an entire team on it as of now, not including us. Everyone in this circle is trusted and were incapable of being any assistance to the Walkers previously. That being said, we cannot, and I repeat *cannot* let what happened just now ever happen again. Delaney, you are not to wander off alone. I'm giving you this whistle I want you to always wear, and you need to alert us if something is out of the ordinary. If you see something you want to explore, take an officer with you and a group. You go nowhere alone, do you understand?" I nodded and took the whistle. I put it around my neck to put his mind at ease. "Okay, now that that's taken care of, I put a sign on Don's front door that says closed for family emergency. Please do not open back up until we get all this sorted out and Justin behind bars, okay?" I nodded again to show I agreed, even though I was really missing Don's. I just wanted a place that was safe and familiar, but his house would do. It was still a part of him that he wanted me to have.

"Now, Lee and Roger please escort Delaney, Lane, and Jace to Delaney's apartment then to Lane's apartment to pack their things to take to their new residence. Make sure you get everything you are going to need for the foreseeable future, okay?" We all nodded in agreement and then Dr. Baker walked in. "Delaney, I have signed your release papers, but the camera stays on and you will need to be restrained while sleeping until you are healed. We can't have you pulling your stitches out or dislocating your arm again while sleeping, understood?" I nodded again.

Looking around that room there were 4 officers, 7 family members, the man I loved, the doctor that loved me, and multiple staff members of the hospital. All of these people were being charged with protecting me, and suddenly a well of anger flooded over me. It was one thing when he was just hurting me, but these people had nothing to do with him. They had no issues with him, and they didn't deserve this. If it came down to it, my mind was made up. This would end with Justin and me. One of us wouldn't walk away from it, but that was how it was going to be. I would not put these people in danger to save myself. It wasn't fair to be put in the position where I needed them to take care of me, and I was growing angrier by the second thinking that this was just another way he could control me. He could be halfway to Mexico by now and laughing knowing that I would never live a normal life until he was behind bars, but I doubted that was the case. It wasn't his style. He would be angry that I hurt Joe and took him out of the picture. He would be angry that I fought back and won twice. He would be angry his friend was behind bars, and I wasn't dead. He had gained nothing, and I had gained my best friend, family, and the support of the police and hospital staff. He wouldn't take that lightly. He would try to finish it himself. I knew this man better than any of these people. This wasn't over, but it was getting close. It was coming to a head, and I wasn't sure I was ready for the outcome, but I knew that I wasn't going down without the fight of my life. That was certain, and I was ready.

# Chapter 12

I let Jace drive the bronco back to the house. Lane was in the backseat with me, and we let Momma have the front seat. Dad, Jamie, and Luke were following us, and behind them was Officer John and Lee with a squad car. Uncle Rex and Greg had gone back at the house to make sure it was all clear before we got there. There was no way to tell if Justin knew about this house or not, but I figured with the police knowing the address, that someone had told him. Jace was thinking the same way, and I could tell by the way he was checking behind us every two seconds to make sure we weren't being followed. I wasn't cleared to drive for at least another week or so, depending on how my arm was feeling. I had a gut feeling that this wasn't going to go on for another week. I couldn't explain it and didn't want to explain it to the rest of them, but my soul was telling me this would be finished one way or another in the next couple of days. I knew Justin's anger, and with Joe out of the picture, he was sure to be angrier than ever.  He wouldn't sit and wait us out, he would come at us all with a vengeance.  That much, I was sure of.

We pulled in and Lane and Jace helped me out of the car.  I was still in the scrubs with nothing underneath, and I really wanted a shower.  Momma shook her head and said that the doc said no shower or bath for another 24 hours at least due to the stitches and the fact they didn't want me raising my left arm over my head to wash my hair.  Momma gathered some clothes for me and looked at me warily.  "D, sweety, I have some wipes I'll give you to freshen up and here are some clothes.  After tomorrow is over you can take a shower, but I need to wash your hair for you.  Please don't fight me on that.  How are you feeling?"  I looked at her, but I couldn't answer honestly.  She would take it personally, and she had suffered enough in the last 24 hours.  "I'm doing fine Momma, just stiff.  Can you grab the anti-inflammatories while you are grabbing the wipes, please?  I've got a killer headache."  Momma nodded quickly and turned to leave me.  Lane was standing there in the doorway and walked in and closed the door behind him.  He gave me a look and told me to lean over so he could pull the scrub top over my head and maneuver it around my arm.  After the top was off, he handed me the hoodie Momma had laid out for me and helped me slip it on then adjusted the sling to fit over the hoodie.  He told me to sit and take the pants off and I did.  He then helped me put on some underwear and sweatpants.  I stood up and pulled the sweatpants the rest of the way up and he cinched them.  I pushed him out of the way and hobbled to the bathroom where I fell to the floor and vomited violently into the toilet.  He grabbed my hair and put it back in a makeshift ponytail to keep it out of my face and ran water over a washcloth and brought it over so I could wash my face.

When I was sure I was finished, I sat back on my butt on the floor of the bathroom and scooted my back up to the wall, pulled my knees up and put my head on them and sobbed. It was like a dam broke and I couldn't stop it. I was sobbing for everyone involved, but mostly sobbing for Lane. He didn't have to be here, and he didn't need to be involved, but I knew he wouldn't have it any other way. In less than a week's time, he had met me all over again and now he was holding my hair up while I wretched in a toilet after getting hit by a car that was driven by a man my ex-husband decided to have kidnap me. How was this okay? How was this what my life had been reduced to? Why was Don the first victim, and why did he have to be a victim at all? I missed him so much my chest felt like someone was sitting on it and forcing the air out of me. I glanced up and saw 4 little eyes staring at me sitting beside Lane on the floor. My Fritz and my new Frank had decided they didn't like it when I cried. I put my legs down and both of them crawled up on me and Fritz took to licking my tears away. I couldn't help but smile. I didn't deserve the undying love that these two little mutts had for me, but I loved them for it so much. Lane sat beside me and pulled me in close to his side, and we loved on the pups for a while.

Momma peeked around the door into the bathroom and saw us on the floor, and instead of asking us to get up, she just joined us. She sat there cross-legged in front of us on the floor and had brought the anti-inflammatories, wipes, and also a few dog treats for the little ones. She leaned forward and cradled my foot in her hands and started massaging it. "D, my love, you have got to quit beating yourself up. We all see it, especially Lane, here. We are all making the choice to stand by you, and you didn't choose for any of this to happen. You didn't ask for it, and you didn't deserve it. You need to remember that. This doesn't all fall on your shoulders, honey. This falls on Justin and Joe's shoulders. They made the choice to take this as far as they have, and they have both got to pay for their crimes. Your Dad and Uncle Rex are already planning with the police that are here, and they will have this place locked up like a fortress before you know it. He won't get to you or any of us. You need to rest and relax and heal. You aren't good to anyone in the state you are in. We need you healthy and able to defend yourself, just in case, but I don't think it will come to that. John says the County Sherriff's Office has joined is as well as the State Police. They will get him. Quit holding all the blame, my dear. The blame doesn't rest on you, do you understand me?"

I looked up with tears still rolling down my cheeks. "Yeah Momma, I understand. But nobody else is dying for me. I'm not going to let it happen. If it comes to it, you all have to let him take me if there is no choice to put him down. I will find a way out, and I will win. He won't beat me again, Momma. You have to believe me that I can fix this if I have to." She smiled her sweet smile and switched to rubbing my other foot. "My child, my heart outside my body, we have no doubts you can handle it. We just don't want you to have to. We are a team and Lane has been adamant this entire time that he will not leave your side. If it comes down to you being taken? You best bet one of us will be taken with you or be right behind you. You have fought this alone for so long, and now? Now, my dear girl, you don't have to, and you never will again. You are so loved, remember that. I didn't raise any idiots or any weak children. You are strong and it's your time to show just how strong until you don't have to be strong anymore. I just hate watching you blame yourself for us being here, so please stop. We are here by choice. There is nowhere else on God's green earth we would rather be."

Lane pulled me closer, and I leaned on his shoulder with Fritz and Frank both curled into my lap beside each other. "I knew they would be fast friends," I said with a smile. Momma and Lane both giggled a little and then Lane got up and reached down to help me gently to my feet. We went into the kitchen with Momma close behind us and I got some water to take the medicine with. Greg and Jamie were in the kitchen with Jace drinking a beer and talking strategy. Jace got up and came over to me and looked down into my eyes. "Sis, I can't tell you how angry I've been at you the last few years. There really aren't words, but I felt like you chose him over your family, and I resented you for it. I see what you were dealing with now, and I'm just sorry I wasn't there to see it at the beginning. I could have saved us all a lot of trouble early on if I would have pushed it." I shook my head and grabbed his beer from him and took a swig. "Jace, there isn't anything you could have done, so quit thinking that way. We have tomorrow and the rest of our lives to make up for all the mistakes we all made the last half decade. So, let's get through this, and then focus on rebuilding what should have never been broken. Sound good?" He nodded and took his beer back showing me a look like he wasn't sure that, after what all had happened, if I should have taken a drink. I smiled at him and shooed him away.

I went to the fridge and grabbed a beer of my own, and then I went out on the back deck with Lane at my side. I sat on the swing and watched the sun sinking into the beautiful sky. "It's gorgeous, isn't it?" I turned to Lane and grabbed his hand and laced my fingers with his. "Yeah, D. It's gorgeous." There was a commotion and it sounded like gravel was being turned up and someone was peeling out of the driveway. Lane grabbed me up and got me inside and sat a chair in the corner and told me to stay there. I heard shouting but couldn't make out any words. Dad came in through the front door with an alert look on his face. "Roger and Damien are down. John and Lee are still here, and a deputy drove out here to alert us. They were posted at Don's, watching for any sign of Justin, and they were both shot in the head by two shooters on both sides of the car at the same time. They must have crouched below the mirrors or something because I have no idea how they weren't seen by two trained officers. They are pulling video from the stores around Don's right now to see what they can see. You need to stay inside and stay down and away from the windows, you hear me? If they are armed, this changes the ballgame. Stay out of sight."

My first thought was "they". How can there still be a "they"? Surely Justin had used up all or most of his resources. He wasn't a friendly person, so why were these people risking their lives to kidnap his ex? What was so special about him hurting me that people joined in and assisted? Were there that many deranged people in the world that two people would take out two

172

police officers in order to commit more felonies on top of that just for Justin's approval? What was he telling people he was doing? There was no way he was telling the truth and getting this kind of support, so what could he possibly be saying to gain the kind of support that he is getting? Adrenaline started pumping and the pain took a backseat.

"I need to see John. Now." Lane looked puzzled but stopped me from standing up and told me to wait there and he would get him and bring him to me. John came into view about two minutes later. He looked tired and beaten, but he was trying not to show it. "John, get Jace and Dad. We need to come at this from a different direction." He nodded and Jace and Dad joined him along with Lane, Jamie, Luke, Mom, and Uncle Rex. "Okay guys, think. How does an escaped felon not only go undetected, but gain followers willing to commit multiple felonies a day to assist him? How does he have a following so deep that they are willing to execute two police officers, stake out a hospital, attempt to run all of us over, and there are still at least two standing? How does someone get that many people behind a cause when that cause is to kidnap an ex-wife that he already failed in killing once?" John looked pensive and then rebutted, "He doesn't. There is no way any sane person would follow in on something like this. There is no way they would pick up the torch unless there is a lot of money involved, which is doubtful, or they are being fed a story that makes it a worthy cause. He is feeding them lies about something, and they are eating it up. Delaney is right. These people are acting like a gang of sorts, and people don't join an anti-police gang for one person's fight. They join because they think they are all in the same fight. What could he possibly be selling them that is worth their lives and futures?"

"That's the big question, John. I have no idea what Justin would even have to offer, but the man is a master manipulator. If there is a way that he could have sold this to others so that it became his thug friends verses the police and left kidnapping me out of it to the majority of them, I could see some idiots taking that challenge on. The company he keeps isn't the best, but they aren't stupid enough for all of them to join in to just try to kidnap a woman they don't even know and have no issue with. He is molding a force to take out the police to leave us as sitting ducks with little to no backup. He wants to smoke us out. Jamie, you used to hang with Joe. Did they know the kind of people that would do something like this? Or could it be people he met in prison that had an axe to grind with the system that had nothing to do with Justin that he could exploit?"

Jamie looked thoughtful, and then it looked like a lightbulb went off. "Justin got close with a group of people from a few towns over that had some issues with law. Their dad was wrongfully convicted and spent the majority of his life and their lives in prison. They overturned the conviction after DNA cleared him and they got him out, but he had already been in about 30 years for a murder he didn't commit. Joe talked about them all the time. The man got out of prison and got killed a few weeks later in a drive-by shooting that all the boys thought was the police cleaning house because they didn't believe he was innocent even after he was cleared. They always had a huge vendetta on the police. The oldest son owned a bar that Justin and Joe would go to all the time in Stillwell, and word had it, the police were not only not welcome in the bar, but if they showed up they wouldn't be served and would be asked to leave. I had forgotten all about that." I nodded slowly and looked into my brother's eyes. "Jamie, this is important. What was the family's name?" All eyes were on Jamie, and he was trying hard to remember.

Dad looked up and said, "I know that story. That's Rodney Lakewood. I don't know his boys' names though. John, do you have a way to look it up?" John looked around and located his tablet and brought it over. He looked up Rodney Lakewood and the story first. Then he searched a little deeper and found the sons' names and searched them in the police database. "They certainly don't look like law abiding citizens. The only one without a felony arrest or an assault arrest is the oldest. There are stipulations on liquor and beer licenses, which is probably why he is the one that owns the bar. The others have offenses ranging from possession, disturbing the peace, resisting arrest, felony assault, felony sexual assault, and the list goes on. I can't put a BOLO out on them as suspects, but I can put a search out on them as persons of interest in the homicide of a police officer, which will get the same results. If they are in the city, our guys will find them. I will also let them know that they could be armed and dangerous and are not to be handled without backup. If we find them and take them in, maybe we will get to the bottom of what's driving these boys to make the biggest mistake of their lives."

I nodded. John looked at me closely and said, "Are you sure you don't want to come to work for me? You seem to have an eye for getting to the root of issues." I smiled and told him I'd think it over after I could walk without grimacing. He nodded and walked off to go watch the door. I know it's a long shot, but in my head, I truly believed we had just cracked this thing wide open.

I looked at Lane and said, "Hey. I'm going to go lay down and rest my eyes without sleeping if I can. The pain is starting to get pretty bad, and I feel like just laying down may help with some of it, okay?" He looked worried but nodded. "I'll go with you and let them handle the house." Lane helped me up and into the bedroom and into the bed. He laid on top of the covers beside me with my head resting on his chest. I didn't want to sleep, not yet and not in restraints. I just wanted a minute of silence so my body could ease up and my brain would kick in and help me figure all of this out. As soon as I closed my eyes an explosion happened that seemed to pick the entire house up and drop it back down. Pictures were flung off the walls, decorations fell off tables, I could hear dishes breaking in the kitchen, windows were shattered, and people were yelling. Lane jumped up and I was right behind him. I grabbed the gun I had been carrying and followed him to the bedroom door. He opened it a crack to be sure it was clear enough, and then we went into the hallway.

In the kitchen, Dad was laying on the ground with different sized pieces of glass stuck in his face and his chest. I went over to him and crouched beside him. It looked like he had been filling a glass of water at the sink when the kitchen window exploded. I jostled him enough to get him to wake up and he pulled his hands up, but I pushed them back down. "Dad, you need to go to the bathroom and look in the mirror and get the glass out. If you need help, Lane will help you." Lane looked me right in the eyes and said, "No. I am not leaving your side." I shook my head wildly to let him know it was not a debate. I knew Dad needed help immediately. "Lane, I've got to go see who else is hurt. Help him, please. I won't leave the house." I could tell Lane was mad about it, but he helped Dad up and started walking him to the hall bathroom.

I looked throughout the kitchen and didn't see anyone else immediately. I turned around the island and saw Luke sprawled out on the floor. I shook him and he woke up and checked himself but couldn't find any real damage. I asked him to go help Lane with Dad in the bathroom. I made my way to the living room and saw John and Jace trying to pick Jamie up off the floor. He had a piece of glass sticking out of his stomach about the size of a cutting board from the big, beautiful bay window looking out across the yard. I told them Dad was with Lane getting fixed up in the hall bathroom so to take Jamie to the half bath off the study and see if they can't bandage him up. Uncle Rex was coming in behind me and his eyes were huge as he looked out across the lawn. I followed his gaze and what I saw was absolutely terrifying.

The RVs had been blown up. Everything they had brought with them was turning to ash before our eyes. That wasn't the worst part. There was a man standing out there holding a sawed-off shotgun to my mother's head. I walked to the window. I had left my gun on the counter in the kitchen when I crouched to help Dad. I wasn't armed. Looking over at Uncle Rex proved he wasn't armed either. The explosion died down a little where I could make out features of the man. It was Justin, there was no doubt. But he had changed drastically. He had lost a lot of weight, gained a lot of muscle, his eyes were cold and empty like there was no life behind them, he was smiling a crazed smile that mad men get before their life ends in the movies, and he had my mother's life in his hands.

"Uncle Rex. Three things need to happen right now. I am trusting you to make them happen. Are you listening to me?" He didn't move his lips but answered. "Yes." I shuffled forward a few steps to take the attention away from my uncle. "My gun is in the kitchen by the sink on the counter. You are going to slowly go get it and cover me. Second thing is that I am going out there to get Momma. Third thing is that he is going to take me. If he doesn't let Momma go, you find a way to put him down. Don't let him take both of us. If you can't find a way, then you follow us." Uncle Rex looked like he was about to be sick. "D, your dad would never forgive me if I let you walk out there." I looked at him square in the eyes. "All things considered, you and I both know that anyone else goes out there and she dies. There is no other choice. Now, I'm going. You keep Lane and them from following me and find a way to get me back. That's the plan now. Get me back."

With that, I held my hands up, walked up where Justin could still see me and sidestepped to the front door. I looked to my right and saw Fritz and Frank crouched under the bed in the master bedroom. "Boys, it ends tonight. I love you. Take care of Lane." I reached down and opened the front door. I stepped out with my arms raised, and Justin's smile grew into a grimace I would never be able to forget. No matter how many hours, days, or years I had left to live.

# Chapter 13

Momma had tears rolling down her face and she was sobbing and speaking but I couldn't hear what was being said. I saw two shadows in the distance but didn't know if they were my people or his, so first thing I needed to do was get Momma to safety. I walked up and stood about 10 feet away.

"Hey, Justin. We all know you came for me, so can you let Momma go, and you and I can finish this together?" He sneered and pulled the gun tighter to Momma's temple as she grimaced and closed her eyes. "Delaney, Delaney. What *we all know* is that you don't get to call the shots anymore. You've lost and you've cost a lot of people their lives and time. You have never been worth the effort these people expended to try to help you. You aren't worth anything at all. I will handle this how I want to handle this, and you don't get a say. In fact, you have lost the right to talk altogether. Keep your mouth shut, or Mrs. Jameson here will die before you do, and I'll draw it out just to make you watch her suffer. Understood?" I looked at Momma and looked up at Justin and nodded.

About that time, several things happened.  The shadows behind Justin shifted and I got a glimpse of Uncle Rex and Jace.  They didn't have a clear shot.  The thing about firearms and using them to protect against intruders or people aiming to do you harm is that you can't just aim and shoot the person.  You take into consideration what's behind them in case the bullet goes straight through.  Mom and I were in direct line with any bullet that would glide through Justin's center mass.  They couldn't shoot at him without the possibility of hurting us in the process.  The other option?  Shooting into the ground behind a person with absolutely no ear protection.  It will stun them and could give you just enough time to get a hostage free, but I doubt the FBI would use that tactic if they didn't have to.  We weren't the FBI.  We were family and we were desperate.  Jace aimed into the ground about 6 feet from his right side and eyed me to make sure I knew what he was planning and used his left hand down by his side to count to three.

Flinching with a gun in your hand held tight against someone's temple is never a good thing.  So, I had to think extremely fast.  I had to get Mom's head out of the line of fire in case he pulled the trigger as he was flinching away from the shot, and I had two seconds to come up with a plan.  In the end, I did what I thought was best.  On the back end of count two, I ran as fast as I could with all the injuries.  I was looking for surprise and I got it.  He flinched away from Mom and started to swing the gun toward me.  Jace's shot rang loud and hard and Justin jumped, but the gun kept coming around.  I slammed my right side into Mom as hard as I could and sent her flying out of the way.  Uncle Rex ran up to grab her and drag her to safety.  Jace let off another ear-piercing shot right behind Justin. I had fallen on the ground beside him, and he reached down and grabbed my hair and pulled me upright by it. He spun with me in front of him, facing my brother, with his gun pointed right at Jace. Jace brought his gun up level about 2 feet to the right of Justin's head. He couldn't be sure to hit him and not hit me, so he was doing it mostly for show.

I screamed for Jace to run and brought my elbow down and caught Justin in the gut as hard as I could. Jace backed off behind a truck where Mom and Uncle Rex had taken cover. Justin recovered from the blow, still with a hand full of my hair, and brought himself upright laughing. That laugh was another thing I would never forget. It was like all the evil was being let out in the open night air  He used my hair like a puppeteer uses strings and kept me between him, the truck, and the house. Guaranteeing that he wouldn't get caught in the line of fire from either, because they wouldn't go through me.

Justin held me there like a ragdoll and spun me around to face the house directly. Through the broken window, I could see Lane standing there with tears streaming down his face. I couldn't die here. Not now. It would kill him. I had to think fast and come up with something. At that minute, Justin started speaking to everyone but me. "The Jameson's. Mighty up on their high horse about to be brought to their knees by one dysfunctional daughter. A broken girl that never really was worth anything to anyone, including them. You left her alone and unguarded for years for me to do as I wished with her, so why would you all care what happens to her now? Rumor has it, you didn't even know about me almost killing her. She didn't trust you enough to tell you that she almost died, did she? She didn't lean on you then. She ruined my life! Did you think I was just going to let her get away with all of that? She helped them take my freedom away! When we got married, we said vows. Until death do us part, and you all gave her to me of your own free will, at least mostly. So, all I'm doing now is taking back what is rightfully mine by law and by God. If you all want her to live, you will call off the dogs. Everything that has happened wouldn't have happened at all if you all would have just let me collect my property and move on, so that blood is on all of you. Not me, my brother, or my friends. So, here is what's going to happen next. Delaney and I are going to leave you here. I have friends in high places, and if I hear of any search or any bulletin or manhunt, she dies. Ya'll have a nice night, now."

With that he gripped my hair closer to the scalp and stuck the butt of his gun into my left shoulder which brought out a guttural scream that I couldn't keep from happening. That made his smile grow bigger as he walked me backwards to his vehicle that he had parked at the end of the driveway. I made eye contact with Lane and the rest of my family that had gathered in the window, and I mouthed "I'm sorry" as we were backing toward the car. He pushed me into the passenger side of the car gripping my bad shoulder to force compliance. My mind was beginning to shut down. It was like a safety switch had been activated and my brain had finally had enough. I couldn't hear anything, wasn't really seeing anything, I was just sitting there waiting for him to get in the driver's seat. I was silently accepting my fate. I had lost.

He got into the driver's seat and sat down and exhaled. He turned to me and grinned. "Leave your seatbelt off sweetheart, this is going to be a short drive." Something in my head flipped that switch back off. This sorry excuse for a man was going to do the same thing all over again and hope that the plate in my head wouldn't hold. He was going to throw me out of a moving car at high speeds and finish what he didn't finish the first time. He was going to make sure I died this time. He just hadn't taken into account the anger that had built up in me. He didn't consider the hatred I had for him. He didn't realize that I now had something so much better to live for. He didn't think through the fact that I had spent the last year making damn sure that this would never happen to me again. The biggest mistake he made was underestimating who I had become since the accident. I knew in that second, he wouldn't win. I had trained for this. I had fought for my chance to take back the power that he took from me that day, and today was my chance. If I died, I was taking him with me.

# Chapter 14

He got the speed up to about 70 mph on the highway headed across town. There was a surprisingly small number of cars on the road, which was perfect for him. He took an exit for a small highway that would take us the long way back to the small town we grew up in. I knew the highway and also knew that it was mostly all wooded area or farms. That meant next to no population and next to no help, even if I could find a way to stop him. The gears kept turning though. My mind wasn't ready to give up, even though my body had seen better days. I needed all the strength I could muster for what was going to come next.

There was a farm that I had visited before with Uncle Rex when I was younger up ahead on the right about 8 miles. If I could get the car stopped or off the road and out of the car, my plan might work. It was dark, and that particular farmer was probably well asleep by this hour. Justin was doing about 60 mph and driving like he had all the time in the world, which worked for me. I needed him relaxed and thinking he was in control. I had about 5 minutes left until we got to the farm, and I needed to be sure it would work, which I almost was. I kept myself calm and faced out the window like I had accepted my fate, which I think made him even happier. He had relaxed his gun hand and it wasn't pointed anywhere but at the floor of the car.

We got to the corner of the property, and I knew it was now or never. Using the reflection in the window as a guide to see by, I turned and grabbed the wheel and jerked right all in a fluid motion too quick for him to react to in time. The farm had many hills throughout it. The car immediately ramped the first one and flung nose first into the second hill and came to a jolting stop. I had braced myself and was holding on to the door handle, but was still thrown yet again into the windshield on my left side, but from the inside of the car this time. The airbag didn't go off, and the windshield cracked but held firmly in place instead of shattering. I couldn't focus on the pain right then, I had to move. The seat had flown forward so I pushed it back and gripped for the handle and forced the door open and fell out onto the ground.

Justin was coming out of shock, and gripping around trying to find the gun, but not finding it. I quit watching and took off across the farm on foot. I was crouched and running as fast as my wounded body would carry me to the place where I knew I had to get him to for the plan to work. It was dark, but I knew I was going the right direction based off the barn in the background. Justin had exited the car and let out a howl like a wild animal. I could hear him rushing behind me following me. The moon was giving my position away, but was also guiding my way, so it was helping and hurting my situation all at the same time.

I knew it had to be close, so I slowed just enough to be sure of my footing. Then I saw it. The old well that had been covered with a few planks of wood level with the ground. Normally, you could walk right over it and not even flinch or notice, but I had wondered what would happen if someone were to fall into the hole last time I visited, and it had stuck in my head. I always had been a curious child with a strange thought process. Now, I was going to get to find out what happened if everything went according to plan, which it would hopefully.

Justin was making his way closer and closer to my location, but thanks to some good fortune, he didn't have the gun in his hand, and he was headed straight for the well. I crouched and carefully slid the wood off the top and pulled it back into the brush with me.

185

"I can see you, Delaney. Why don't you stand up and face me? You seem to think you have this all figured out and you are going to walk away, but I can guarantee you that isn't going to happen. This ends tonight, and it ends for you forever." I stood and faced him and backed up a couple of paces trying to get him to come forward. "Justin, why don't you just come on over and end it, then? Are you scared of me when you don't have a gun pointed at my face or my Momma? Not so tough when you aren't armed, are you?" I knew that would set a fire in him, and it worked. He took off at a dead sprint toward me, and about that time a gunshot went off from behind him. I saw the bullet hit Justin in the shoulder the same time that his foot was no longer on solid ground, and he disappeared before my eyes. I looked up and saw Greg holding the gun and shaking. He was beaten up badly.

Justin hit the bottom of the well with a slight splash and a scream of agony. He had probably broken both of his legs, because according to the farmer the well only had a couple of feet of rain in it at any given time due to a drain going out to the crops. Basically the rainwater fell in, went through the drain, and watered the crops on this side of the barn for him. I put my hand up to stop Greg from coming any further, and I stepped up and looked down the hole. I could see Justin's face down there and I knew he was in pain, and that was about the most satisfying sight I had seen in my lifetime. I looked back up at Greg.

"Stay there. I'll come around to you. I took the wood off the top of the well." Greg sat down in the brush and put the gun down beside him. "How did you get here so fast?" I asked. He looked up at me, trying to catch his breath. "I hid in the trunk when the explosion happened. I figured one way or the other he was going to be walking away with at least one of you with him, and I couldn't let that happen without trying to stop it. I left the back seat gapped so I could kick it open to get through or to shoot, whichever needed to come first. Then the car wrecked, and I was thrown through the seat into the back of your seats. I just stayed as still as I could, and he took off so fast after you that he didn't even see me, so I followed. How the hell did you know that well was even there?" I breathed a sigh of relief and laughed. "Your dad brought me out here when I was young to help bail hay. I saw the well and curiosity got the better of me and I started asking a ton of questions. Mostly, I was worried about safety, but Uncle Rex and Old Man Staton didn't seem to think twice about it. Do you have your phone?" Greg reached into his pocket and produced a cell phone.

I dialed Officer John by memory, and he answered before the first ring ended. "Hey John, it's Delaney. We have a situation here that is going to require some law enforcement and some finesse. Justin is in an old well on a farm that my Uncle Rex can get you to. It's Mr. Staton's. He's alive and unarmed, but both of his legs are probably broken, and Greg shot him as he was going down. You will probably have to bring a fire truck to get him out. Also, could you see if Uncle Rex could call and wake Mr. Staton up and let him know we are here? I don't want him to come out shooting." John let out a little relieved laugh and he said, "Yes ma'am, on it." And with that, he disconnected the line.

About 5 minutes later, Mrs. Staton came running with Mr. Staton in tow through the field toward the well in her nightgown.  She got to us and looped me up in a big hug and then pulled Greg in, too.  Then she started assessing our injuries and herding us both back to the house to get cleaned up and stitched up, if needed.  I forgot why I love country people so much until that night.  She raised hell and woke 3 of the neighbors up.  All the men went out to the well to watch Justin until the first responders got there.  They didn't want any chance of him leaving, so they all had shotguns just in case he somehow sprouted wings.  Mrs. Staton and the rest of the wives were fussing over Greg and I like we were royalty.  They got us fresh clothes, a couple of them took me aside and tried to re-bandage what they could and assess whether they thought anything was broken.

The police showed up first at just under 20 minutes with my entire family squeezed in the bronco following them with a little red flashing light on the dash that I'm assuming Officer John let them borrow to get them through traffic at the heels of the police.  They all stopped on the road where the car had run off and into the small hill.  I could see my family pouring out and swiftly making their way toward the house.

The firefighters got there soon after and due to the hills, they couldn't get their trucks through, so they had to send a stretcher down that Justin had to strap himself to in order to be brought up.  I don't think it hurt their feelings to watch him suffer just a little longer.  The farmers were waiting there with their shotguns to be sure he didn't try to run for it, but that turned out to be a wasted effort like I had suspected.  It didn't look like Justin's legs were ever going to work right again, even if the doctor's put in their best effort.

I walked out onto the porch as Officer John and my family came up to greet me. Momma grabbed me and hugged me and sobbed. Lane stood back and let her have her turn, but as soon as she let me go, he posted at my side with me under his wing, and I don't think I left his sight for the next two weeks, even though the threat was technically over.

Officer John stepped up. "Delaney, you were right about the Lakewood boys. They were waiting at Justin's house for you all to get there. They, in short, were planning to assist with getting rid of your body by the looks of things. We will get their full statement tomorrow, but for now they are being detained. We also found out which officers and personnel had helped Justin escape, but I can debrief you on that later. We need to get you back to the hospital to get fixed up and then get you home. Does that sound okay?"

I nodded. I finally felt like everything was finally coming to an end. Everything was finally working out. It had been the longest road to get to this point, and so much was gained and lost in these past few weeks, but everything was going to be okay. We were going to come out on top. This was the new beginning that we had hoped and dreamed of.

# Chapter 15

Surprisingly enough, I didn't have many "new" injuries from the events. My old ones were pretty angry at me, but I looked to be on the mend. Dr. Baker had forcefully made me stay 2 nights for observation, just to be sure. She walked into the hospital room as I was getting on my clothes to leave. "Delaney, I don't usually get personally involved in my patients lives. I don't usually make house calls, set up video surveillance, or come to the hospital every time one of my patients gets injured. Nothing about my time with you has been usual in any sense of the word, and I wanted to tell you why. My daughter, Ariana, went through a similar situation as you. She fought hard, but she couldn't keep the demons at bay. I lost her 3 years ago from an overdose. It almost killed me trying to help her and then it almost killed me when she gave up. I could not watch the same thing happen to you, and not do something about it to make it right. You are an extraordinary woman with a heart that is so big, and all I wanted was to get *you* to see that. You seemed to be the only one that couldn't. I don't think there is a need for you to see another therapist. I think you are going to be just fine if you lean on and accept the support of the people who have proven their love to you over and over again these past few weeks. Don't go backwards, Delaney. Only move forward, and make sure that you keep your people close to you in the process."

"Doc, can I ask you a personal question?" Dr. Baker looked a little stunned but nodded her head to indicate yes. "What is your first name?" Dr. Baker smiled and looked down, then back up to meet my eyes. "Out of all I just talked to you about, your only question is my first name?" I smiled and nodded my head. "I'll explain after you tell me what it is." She nodded, slowly, again, and replied, "Madison. Madison Baker is my name."

"Before all my family came back into my life with Lane, Don and I would talk. I counted Don as a friend and my dog as a friend, but for some reason my brain computed that I couldn't count you as a friend without knowing your first name. So now, Madison, just know that you are in my circle too. You have done just as much for me throughout all of this as my family has. You have been there rooting me on for the last year and keeping me sane, even if I fought you on it at every turn. You never gave up on me. You believed in me. I can guarantee you that your daughter knew that you believed in her too. She did what she could, and she fought through as far as she could go, but she knew every step of the way that you had her back, because I've known it as well. Even when I was fighting you with everything I had. Thank you, Madison Baker, for being one of my 3 friends back when it was just Don, Fritz, and you." Dr. Baker looked up with tears in her eyes, crossed the room, and pulled me into a gentle hug. "Delaney, any time you need anything, I'll be here. Lane? Take her home please. She's beginning to look like a frequent flyer at the hospital." Lane laughed from his corner by the window, came over and took my hand and led me to the door for my *hopefully* last exit from this place for a while.

Lane was driving me home and about halfway there he threw a black bandana at me. "Roll that up and blindfold yourself, please. I've got something to show you." I smiled and started rolling the bandana, then tied it around my eyes. We pulled in and I could hear some rustling but couldn't make out what was happening. Lane came around my side of the Bronco, opened the door, and lifted me out and to the ground carefully. He led me for a few feet, then told me to stop and stand there. I was smiling so big. I had no idea what he was doing, and I didn't care. We were okay and everything was going to be okay. I felt some hands at the back of my head as someone took the bandana off.

When my eyes re-focused to the brightness, I saw a huge banner on the front of my house that said "Welcome Home Delaney" in huge letters. The entire police force plus some people from back home and all my family were there smiling and cheering. They had streamers all over the place and silly string draping over everything. All the windows had been fixed and the bombed RVs had been towed away. Then the "Welcome Home Delaney" sign fell away, and a new sign stood in its place. It said "Delaney, will you marry me?" and I looked over to see Lane dropping to one knee in front of me on the grass. He opened a box and my Great Grandmother's wedding ring glistened under the beautiful sun at me. Mom must have gotten it for him and had it cleaned when he most likely asked them for my hand along with their blessing. I smiled and laughed and said, "Yes!". The crowd went crazy, and more streamers came out, noise makers were going off, more silly string was being strewn everywhere. Lane put the ring on my hand, got up, and gave me a huge welcome home kiss, then held me in his arms for a minute. He begrudgingly lowered me back down to Earth, and the crowd turned to talking to each other.

I looked up to see Dad making his way to me with 3 beers in his hand being held by their necks. He walked up and handed one to Lane and one to me. "Kids, I don't know that I've ever been this happy for a couple in my entire life. You all have had to fight through things that most people don't have to fight through in their entire lives in the last few weeks, and Lane, you never wavered. Delaney, you never quit trying to take care of him and he never quit trying to take care of you. It was the easiest decision of my life to give Lane my blessing to ask for your hand. Your Momma and I will always be here for both of you, through all the hard times, and I guarantee you, there will be more hard times. Just hopefully nothing to this extreme. Please make sure you remember that we will always have your back and always have your best interest in mind. Also, big news, we all are going to move up here close to you. Officer John over there got us a good deal on some land, and we are going to move the farm up here. Jace, Jamie, and Luke are making the move too. They want to be close by to see if there are any kiddos of yours that they can corrupt in the future. What do ya'll say to that? Ready to make a new town our hometown? Lane and I laughed and then I grabbed Daddy into a bear hug. I couldn't have been happier.

Momma came out moments later. She had been waiting hand and foot on the guests and enjoying every minute of it. Officer John was following behind her. They arrived at almost the same time, and Officer John stepped up. "Delaney, we got all the officers involved as well as the inside guys in the prison. We also got the Lakewood boys. None of them are getting off easy. The DA is throwing the book at every single one of them for turning our justice system inside out for their own personal gain. Turns out that Justin had some blackmail on the officers and used it to gain their help on the inside.  Everything has been sorted, charges have been filed, and nobody will walk away with less than 20 years.  Justin looks like he will be looking at the death penalty.  He has been released from the hospital after a double amputation.  They couldn't fix his legs, so they took them.  He won't be able to escape ever again.  You and Lane will have a happy care-free life ahead of you where Justin is concerned.  You both deserve it.  I also have several job openings and the mayor has agreed to waive the college requirement for you if you are interested.  So, take some time off, then come find me if you want it.  If not, I'll be frequenting Don's to check up on you.  Until then, I'll let you all celebrate.  I have a lot of paperwork to fill out."  He came forward and gave me a quick hug and shook Lane's hand for congratulations and walked off toward his squad car. The other officers saw their leader leaving and decided to follow suit, but all swung by to offer congratulations before leaving.

Momma hugged both of us and led us back to the house.  She had made an entire buffet of food and was going to make sure we sampled one of everything. Mr. and Mrs. Staton were there as well and came up to offer their congratulations and told me that they weren't filling in the well in case I ever needed to use it again, then winked and walked off smiling.  Lane laughed so much in the next few hours that I found myself in awe of his happiness.  I couldn't take my eyes off of him.  Of all the ways for our story to end, this beginning to our life together was one I hadn't even tried to imagine.  But here we were.  Life was officially starting over for the both of us, and this time we were going to get to do it all together.

# Chapter 16

Six years later was the day that would change everything and change nothing all at once. I made a lunch for our two kids to take with them to Uncle Jace's house. I got my beautiful baby boy and my perfect 4-year-old daughter up out of bed like every other day since the day they were born. I gave them a bath one at a time and then handed them off to Lane for him to dress them. They looked absolutely beautiful when he brought them downstairs. My heart had never been so full.

I gave Lane a huge hug, then my baby girl a kiss and scooped my boy up in my arms and just held him and breathed him in for a minute. Today was going to be a hurdle and a reminder of what I had gone through, but I wouldn't let any ounce of that roll off onto our children. I had made that perfectly clear to Lane as well. Today was just another day except they get to go spend it with their Uncle Jace and I'm sure half the family will be there as well waiting for us to get back. The evil that was in our past was going to stay there, apart from that day. The last day we would ever have to think of any of the terror that happened to us unless we chose to. Nobody would ever force our hands again.

We dropped them off, got a quick hug from Jace and took off for the city. We stopped by the precinct and picked up Officer John. He pointed us to where we needed to go, and we followed his directions. I had gotten dressed up for the occasion. I wore a bright coral colored dress with black print on it and black heels. Lane wore a coral shirt to match, nice jeans, and black shoes. We looked like we were headed for church, but it was quite the opposite.

We pulled up and the guard showed us through, and we were escorted to a waiting room. A different guard came in and told us all that we could expect to see and experience during the execution. Today was the day that the State of Oklahoma put the reason for all my night terrors to rest for good. Today was the day that Justin would die. I found myself not feeling much of anything. I was numb to the entire concept, even though I didn't really relish the thought of someone being put to death before my eyes, Justin had ceased to be a living human in my eyes long ago. I promised myself I wouldn't lose sleep no matter what happened, because the decision had been made by the State. I hadn't asked them to kill him, I had just been a witness to the crimes against me and they had come up with that solution all on their own. I didn't disagree with their solution, but I didn't agree with it either. Again, I just felt nothing.

Lane and I found our seats inside the viewing chamber. They asked if Justin had any last words, and he looked into the one-way glass separating the chamber from where he sat. I knew he couldn't see me; they had informed me of that before this process began, but my blood still ran cold when he looked directly ahead, seemingly directly into my eyes and said, "Leave your seatbelt off sweetheart, this is going to be a short drive." My lungs didn't fill with air, it was like they didn't want to work at all. Lane squeezed my hand, and my body reacted by allowing me oxygen. They administered the injection, and for once, Justin was right. It was short. Seemed too sudden and seemed like there should have been more suffering, but I guess in his way, he had suffered quite a bit along the way as well.

We walked out into a sunny day with Officer John and invited him to coffee at Don's. We all went to Don's together and walked in to find Luke and Jamie with a full house. I went behind the counter and offered my assistance, but Luke waived me off. I went to the coffee pot, poured three coffees, and put them on a tray to take to our table. We sat there and talked about the past like it wasn't a nightmare for all of us. Then we talked about how far we had come and how amazing things had turned out, and we all smiled, laughed, and enjoyed our time together, almost as if we hadn't just watched a man die.

There were no words to explain how it felt to be in that room and watch what I watched that day. No amount of tears, hopes, or dreams that would keep me from worrying myself sick that something like that could happen to our children. Our beautiful, innocent babies weren't going to be babies forever. I vowed that day that nobody would ever harm a hair on their head. Not if I could still breathe, walk, and fight. My babies would never have to endure the life that I had to endure before I found the life that I deserved. They would grow up on the farm. They would learn to shoot. They would learn right from wrong, and I would die before anything ever came between them and the lives they deserved.  And I had an army of a family there to fight right alongside me on their behalf.

The night terrors were over.  The nightmare was over.  That day would be the 2nd new beginning to Lane and my lives, and this one would be taking place in a world without Justin in it.  We were going to be just fine, and we were going to protect our children with everything we had until our dying day.

### Acknowledgements

*I want to thank my amazing husband for always pushing me to continue with this story and showing me how important it was to make this book a reality for me. Without you, I'm not sure I would have accomplished this, and I will always remember the role you played in making this book complete.*

*To my Mother-in-Law "Bonus Mom" Tammy: You believed in the book from the beginning, and always proof-read and edited any time I needed it.  You were my number one cheerleader, and I cannot thank you enough for supporting my dream from day one.*

*I want to thank my childhood friends Becca and Haley for reading, editing, and assisting with pulling this book together to help it flow better.  You all are amazing, and life would be dull without you both.*

*I want to thank my Memaw and my sister Kate for reading the book and believing in me and offering words of encouragement along the way, along with my parents. Without you pushing me to be the best I can be, I don't know that this book could have happened.*

*To my coworkers Cacy, Mac, Sara, and Jess: you all are amazing. You believed in me from day one and have pushed me constantly to better my life and my career. You all play a big role in the success that I have achieved this far, and I can't thank you enough for that. Dottie, Tonya, and Katie: you all have been great mentors and pushed me along the way to never give up and always push to be the best I can be, and I will always cherish that as well. Thank you all for everything.*

*Without a village of people, some unnamed, this book wouldn't have become a reality for me, and I owe each and every one of them my gratitude. Thank you all for believing in me.*